# Shadows of the Apocalypse

## The Beginning

## Vince Byrd

Shadows of the Apocalypse
The Beginning
Book One

Copyright by: Vince Byrd
2017

Scripture quotations taken from the King James Version.

This is a work of fiction. Any names, characters and events are fictitious. The author took artistic liberties with places, locations, towns, vehicles, items and buildings.

While places and buildings maybe real, they were used in a purely fictional manner.

ISBN: 978-0692948231

# ACKNOWLEGEMENTS

I want to thank my wife Angie, for her faith and confidence in me. When mine wavered, hers stood strong. She always encouraged me to go on. I enjoyed the countless hours we spent discussing and bouncing ideas around while I was writing, and we were editing this book. You are my inspiration and I draw from our own love story for some of the characters in this book.

I also want to thank my daughter, my English Major, and now a big time editor, Sara Ashlyne Byrd who spent hours editing this project for me, and for her creative wit. Without her, this book might have been a train wreck.

Thank you Katie, for an awesome cover design, you nailed it on the first try. And thanks to my format genius and all that contributed to this project.

*Dedicated to our Creator for giving us the minds to think and dream.*

*May we always think to dream.*

# Chapter 1

It was a cold December day when flight 829 left from Niagara International Airport bound for Atlanta. Little did the passengers know of the fate that was before them. It started out a normal day like any other, except life and death had become a coin toss, who lived and who died.

The 737 vibrated and swayed after a thunderous explosion outside of Jesse Gibson's window. One engine was lost, and the plane plunged downward, quickly losing altitude as the passengers' breath was swept away with surprise. A second engine burst into flames; red lights flashed and beeping noises were heard throughout the plane. The pilot announced over the intercom, "We're going down! Prepare for impact!" Fire blazed in the engine cowlings on the wings outside as the oxygen masks dropped from compartments in the ceiling. Each passenger grabbed one and placed it on their heads and over their faces. The plane continued to plummet until tree tops came into view. A flight attendant gave quick instructions to lean forward and make sure everyone was strapped in tight as she struggled to find her seat. The plane finally leveled out a bit then dipped down and rocked side to side as the pilot tried to gain some kind of control.

The man sitting beside Jesse grabbed his arm and said, "I am a U.S. marshal, take this card, if I don't make it contact this man. He'll know what to do."

Jesse took the card, looked at it briefly and said loudly through his mask, "For what? I mean, why?" He shoved it into his shirt pocket with a bewildered look on his face while the plane dipped down again. Jesse turned his thoughts to his children Jacob and Paige, and the times they'd shared together. The plane rotated hard to the left as everyone feared for their lives. "Please God, I'm not ready," Jesse whispered a prayer.

With a loud crack and a ferocious jolt, Jesse was shaken around like a man-sized ragdoll on a roller coaster as the plane's left wing struck the tree tops. Screams and breaking noises invaded his ears as he tried to cling to the seat in front of him. The shifting direction of each impact caused him to lose grip on anything he tried to hold onto. Carry-on luggage was tossed about the cabin, and he felt a couple bump off his back. He felt a giant gust of cold air as the floor of the fuselage bounced erratically under his feet. Several tree branches pierced through windows then the plane came to a sudden stop, like someone stomped on the brakes, flinging Jesse's body forward then back again.

Jesse smelled fresh pine as he took in a deep breath, opening his eyes to look around at the damage. He removed his mask and saw wires dangling from the ceiling and debris all around. One of the flight attendants was limp in her seat unconscious, as a few other passengers began to moan and move their heads. Jesse looked down at the marshal, noticing a piece of shrapnel protruding from the man's neck. He checked for a pulse and found none. He pushed the Marshal back on his seat to get a look at his face. He grimaced at the metal piece that had pierced through the man's cheek. At that moment, he noticed the whole back half of the fuselage was missing, and the crash had left a huge trail of broken pine trees and branches in its wake. He glanced down at the marshal's waist and saw a pistol holstered inside his belt. He quickly unbuckled, reached down, and grabbed the pistol and holster, tucking them into his belt as he stood up. He assessed what was left of the plane for immediate dangers such as fire, flood and threats of an explosion. The plane was still, on the ground, but a little un-level and the wings had been torn off. No more lights flashed and there was no visible fire or smoke.

"Help, I need help!" a woman's voice shouted from about three rows up. Jesse quickly made his way toward the voice as he climbed over carry-on luggage mixed with a few pine branches and the airline's food cart lodged between the rows on its side.

"Are you hurt?" Jesse asked the woman struggling with her seatbelt.

"I'm not sure. I can't get this belt undone," she replied.

"Okay, my name is Jesse. Let me have a look at you real quick to see if you're hurt. You have a trail of blood trickling from your hairline just above your forehead." He looked her over and noticed how beautiful she was with her bronzed skin, green eyes, and curly, auburn hair. "Are you okay, does your head hurt; are you dizzy?"

"Besides the fact we just fell from the sky and I might've peed myself, my head hurts a little but no, I'm not dizzy," she cracked off.

"Looks like you are shaking a little, and I know it's cold, but I want you to look at me and take a couple of deep breaths," Jesse instructed. She began to breathe in deeply. "Good, that's it, let it out. We are safe now and the plane has stopped." She formed a semi smile as her eyes locked with his, and she began to feel safe and calm again. She sensed a spiritual purity in his brown eyes and felt very comfortable looking into them. She was pleased at his rugged look with three-day-old stubble which complimented his chiseled face, broad shoulders, and chestnut wavy hair. He smiled back at her and said, "Let me see if I can set you free." He tugged on the belt latch, but it would not budge. He climbed up on the seat next to her for a better grip. He pulled with greater effort, and it unlatched finally. He slipped and fell toward her, catching himself just before he smacked into her. Their faces were just an inch away, feeling one another's breath and he said, "I'm sorry, I didn't get your name?"

"Kat," she whispered. My name is Katy, but everyone calls me Kat."

"Well Kat, you're loose from your belt, and you have a little bump on your head," he reassured.

"Oh, but other than that I'm fine?" she responded.

"You look fine to me," he said as his face reddened a little. "I'm sorry; I just realized how that sounded. I meant you look good... I really mean you have no broken bones and medically speaking, you're fine. You might have a mild concussion but nothing to worry about. But I think you are going to have to push me back up, so I can regain my balance," he said. She put her hands up, hovering over his muscular pecks and second-guessed their position. She looked him in the eye, and he nodded his head yes. She proceeded to touch his chest and gave him a push. He regained his footing, and they both grinned at each other as another voice screamed, "Help!"

Jesse turned to check the pulse of a man sitting across the aisle from Kat. Kat asked, "Is he...?"

Jesse nodded, and the man that screamed for help screamed again, "Please, please help me!" Jesse climbed back over the cart and bags a couple of seats back, on the other side of the aisle, and was met by another man and woman. A tree branch protruded from the window, pinning a passenger down who was bent over next to the window and impaled the man in the aisle seat that had yelled for help. Jesse saw that the branch was sticking into the man's side, and he was gasping for air. "Hel-Hel-Help me," he puffed looking up at Jesse.

"I need to unbutton your shirt to look at your side, okay?" Jesse asked the impaled man. "You two! Your names please, quickly?" he asked the couple that met him there.

"Hugo and this is Shu," Hugo introduced.

"Hugo, pull his jacket back, but be careful not to move him or the branch," Jesse directed.

"Hey! Get me out of here!" the man pinned under the branch screamed as he started to wiggle around.

"Hey buddy, please don't move. The guy beside you is injured pretty bad, and I need you to be still. There's a tree branch in this man's gut, and if you move, it could kill him. Are you okay?" Jesse asked.

"Yeah, but I need to sit up. I'm a little claustrophobic," the man said. Kat came up from behind and touched Jesse's back.

"Kat, can you talk to this guy and keep him calm?" Jesse motioned toward the guy next to the window. Kat nodded back and slipped in behind the guy's seat.

"His eyes are rolling back into his head. Do something!" Shu said urgently. The impaled man began to gurgle on his own blood, shaking his head and thrashing his arms.

"He's drowning!" Jesse said, as he looked around quickly to find something to use. Seeing a pen in Hugo's shirt pocket, he grabbed it; unscrewed the center, removing the ink refill, clip, and push button; and screwed it back together. "Cover your face," he ordered the guy bent over next to the window. He ripped the impaled man's shirt open, ran his fingers down his ribcage near the tree branch, and stabbed the man in the side of his chest. The pen inserted about halfway spitting out air and blood all over the pinned man's side and back.

The impaled man sucked in a deep breath and then relaxed. He closed and opened his eyes and said in a low, scratchy voice, "Thank you."

"Look Sir, you have a serious injury, probably a hemothorax, which means you're bleeding internally, and there is no way to stop it without immediate surgery. You have already lost a lot of blood," Jesse said, looking up. Seeing three more men gathered in the aisle and on seats nearby looking on, he asked, "Is anyone a doctor?" No one answered, as they looked around at each other. Jesse looked at

Kat; she was rubbing the bent over man's back, keeping him calm and watching Jesse with worry on her face. Jesse placed his hand on the man's shoulder and said, "Sir I'm sorry, but you are going to die. Is there anything you would like for me to say to a loved one when we make it back to Atlanta?" Jesse watched the man's expression change from relief to fear and then to sadness.

"Will... I'm William Gray," he muttered softly. "I was flying back from spreading my wife's ashes over Niagara Falls," Pausing to cough a couple of times, he continued, "My Abigail passed away six months ago of ovarian cancer, and we have no children. She was my life and now, I guess, I'll be joining her soon." Everyone's head drooped a little from the sad news. "Is there a minister here?" he asked with a look of desperation.

"Here! I'm a minister. Reverend Henry Tucker," a voice came from behind. The tall African American elderly man made his way up to William as Jesse stepped back to make way. "What can I do for you, Friend?" There was no reply. "Mister?" There was still no reply. "William?"

Jesse reached over to check William's pulse. "He's gone." A quiet moment passed without anyone saying anything. Jesse looked at Kat, seeing tears running down her face.

Reverend Tucker placed his hand on William's face, closed his eyelids and said, "Rest easy, Friend. Rest easy."

"Hey! What about me?" the man bent over under the branch blurted out.

"Okay, we got you," Jesse replied as everyone began to adjust their positons to make way to get the man out. "I'm going to pull William off the branch and then we'll shove the branch back out the window. Kat, Hugo, lift up on the branch as we pull William so we don't scratch—I'm sorry, what's your name?

"Larry," the man said.

"So we don't scratch Larry's back," Jesse continued. "You got it?" Kat and Hugo both agreed. "Reverend, you might want to move out of the way," Jesse suggested out of respect so Reverend Tucker didn't have to handle the dead. "Shu, grab hold of his jacket and help me pull." Shu shook her head and backed up. Jesse pointed to one of the men and said, "Sir, can you help me with this?"

"Jon," he said. Jon squeezed by Shu, stumbling on the debris in the aisle. He quickly regained his balance and took his place by Jesse, grabbing hold of William's jacket.

"Here we go," Jesse said. They pulled William off the branch and slowly laid his limp body down in the aisle. Kat and Hugo lifted the pine branch up and shoved it out the window as it snagged a couple of times on the way out.

Larry straightened up and said, "About time. Wow! That feels better," he loosened his seat belt, stood up, and turned around. "Holy crap!" he exclaimed, seeing the back half of the plane missing. He proceeded to the aisle careful not to step on or stumble over William, making his way out of the halved-plane. Everyone just watched Larry as he exited, then turning back to one another they just looked at each other, then down at William.

"Ugh…" the limp flight attendant moaned as everyone turned their focus on her. She perked up as Jesse made his way over to her.

"Are you hurt?" Jesse asked.

"No. I think I'm alright, just a little sore," she answered unbuckling her seat belt.

"Let me help you up, Ginger," Jesse said, reading her name tag. He put his hand out, and she took it and stood up.

"Let's check on the pilots," Jesse prompted. He opened the door to the cockpit with difficulty, seeing the pilots were both dead. The nose of the plane had struck a large tree, causing it to stop abruptly.

Several branches had penetrated the cockpit windows, but he checked their pulses anyway to confirm what he already suspected.

"Oh, my! Are they... dead?" Ginger asked, putting her hand over her mouth while tearing up. She saw more deceased, including her coworker Jane, the other flight attendant. Jane's neck was bent in an unnatural way, indicating very clearly she was dead.

"Yes, I'm afraid so," Jesse responded. "I'm sorry about your friends. You have a first aid kit and a medical kit on board, right?" Jesse asked.

"Yes," Ginger answered, as she tried to compose herself, knowing it was still an emergency situation and things need to be addressed. "We have two first aid kits and a medical kit that has a stethoscope, several drugs, and a defibrillator." She grabbed the two first aid kits from a compartment in the galley and the medical bag and handed one to Jesse. "Let's all exit the back of the plane." Everyone stepped out of the huge gaping hole in the halved fuselage and gathered together several yards away.

As Jesse followed Ginger, he passed by the deceased U.S. marshal on his way out. He checked the marshal's pockets for an extra ammo clip, which he found and tucked it into his own. As he was searching, he found some papers and glanced at them, reading the highlighted areas: *Jack Lucas and Jon Lucas to be transported on commercial airlines for extradition on charges of drug trafficking and auto theft in Atlanta, GA.*

Ginger stopped, looked back, and saw Jesse reading the papers and said "He was a U.S. marshal. We were transporting two criminal suspects, Jack and Jon something. Jane pointed out the marshals to me when I came on board."

"Lucas, Jack and Jon Lucas, for drug trafficking. They are brothers and here are their mug shots. They are the two men standing right over there," Jesse reported, pointing out toward the group.

"They don't look like brothers, one with blonde hair and the other with black," Ginger observed.

He folded the papers and shoved them into his back pocket. "You said 'marshals,' was there another on board?" Ginger nodded as she wiped her nose and face with her hands. "Do you see him around?" She shook her head. "Let's not tell anyone about this. We don't want to alarm anyone or spook Jack or Jon." Ginger agreed, as they stepped out of the plane.

# Chapter 2

"Our cell phones are all dead, do you have one?" Kat asked Jesse.

Jesse reached into his right front pants pocket and pulled out his cell phone, replying, "Yeah, mine's dead too." He tried the power button but the phone didn't come on. "That's really weird. No one's phone is working?"

"No, none of them," Hugo answered.

"Wait, where's Larry?" Jesse asked the group. Hugo pointed over to the side where they were all standing. "Larry, have you checked your cell phone?" Jesse asked, as Larry turned while zipping up his pants after just relieving himself only a few feet away from everyone.

"Yes, I have, and nothing, just a black screen. When do you think help will get here? I have a business meeting this evening," Larry responded.

Jesse and Kat looked at one another and both raised their eyebrows. "Not sure," Jesse answered. He turned to Ginger and asked, "Okay, you are the last survivor of the crew and that makes you in charge. What do you want us do now?"

Ginger put up her hands and said, "I don't know; I'm still in shock. This was my first assignment as a flight attendant, and Jane was my supervisor. We trained and trained on how to serve, address emergencies on the plane, but once the plane is down and the people are out, the emergency crews are supposed to be here to take over. This airline took pride in never having a crash. What do you suggest?"

"I think we should take the first aid kits and search for more survivors and help them. After that, we should gather items for the night. If help is not here by then, it's going to get colder, so we want to be prepared. Plus, figure out something for everyone to eat later, to keep our strength up," Jesse suggested.

"That sounds good, let's do that," Ginger agreed. "The airline did say if we're ever in an emergency landing, and we have to vacate the plane, everyone should stay together.

"Emergency landing, that's an understatement," Larry jabbed.

"Yeah, still, let's do this together, everyone agree?" Everyone was in agreement and if help did arrive they would all be in the same place.

"How about we spread out though and walk the crash area, keeping within sight of everyone. If you find someone alive, call out. Ginger has the medical kit; I have a first aid kit and if someone else wants to take one, we have another," Jesse suggested.

"I'll take one," Hugo replied and reached out to Ginger. Ginger handed him the kit, and they began their search.

Plane fragments and chunks of the wreckage stretched out for about a half a mile. Black and white smoke could be seen in the distance, and both wings had been ripped off by huge pine treetops. The tail end of the plane was upside down about half way from where the first wing ended up and where the front half of the fuselage had stopped. Both wings were on fire as well as the area around them from the fuel spillage, but one was nearly burned out. There were snow patches all around, and the ground was still a little frozen so the fire hadn't spread to the foliage much outside the fuel spillage surrounding what was left the by plane. There were several empty seats scattered about the site as well as luggage and clothes blowing in the breeze upon the ground. Gruesome sights of a couple of dozen mangled bodies were strewn around the length of the scene.

"Jon! Quick, over here," Jack whispered loudly to his brother as the others were distracted by more of the dead. Here's the other marshal. Let's get his gun." The marshal was lying face down in the dirt. His jacket was half ripped off with a heavily blood–stained, light-blue shirt under it. He had a gaping wound on his left shoulder and a large contusion on his neck. Jack reached down while glancing around to see if anyone was looking at him and tugged on the marshal's pistol. The marshal groaned and tried to roll over on his back. Jack quickly withdrew his hand and then helped push him on over.

The marshal looked up at him and said in a low, strained voice, "Help me."

Jack grabbed Jon's arm and pulled him over a few inches to block the view from the others as Jack grabbed a piece of clothing nearby and shoved into the marshal's mouth. He then punched the marshal in the throat several times as he watched the marshal gag and gasp for air.

"Jack! Are you crazy? I'm not going down for murder too," Jon whispered forcefully.

"Don't you see little Bro, we're free once he's dead. No one else knows about us. We can leave and be free again," Jack responded.

"Boy, sometimes I think I'm adopted. Don't you think that sweet, young redhead knows about us?" Jon remarked about Ginger.

"That's alright. We'll get her too but we'll and have some fun with her first," Jack said, watching the life drain from the marshal.

"You are always doing stupid stuff that just gets us in deeper. We can just leave and forget about her. Look where we are, man. We're in the backwoods of who knows where, probably miles from anywhere, in the middle of Appalachia." Jon reached down and grabbed the pistol and said, "I'll hang on to this or else you might go postal on someone. I mean it, Jack; you're not touching that hot, little gingy. We're leaving as soon as we can. I figure help won't be here for at least several hours. It will be dark soon, let's slip away then grab some food from the plane and go. It will be awhile before anyone realizes we're gone."

Jack removed the clothing from the marshal's mouth and tossed it to the side. They both moved on like nothing was wrong and the marshal was already dead.

No one was found alive as far as anyone knew until they all reached the tail. There were several passengers still strapped in and upside down. Jesse and Hugo rushed in to help, followed by Kat and Ginger tromping on the ceiling, which was now the floor, of the back half of the cabin. "She's alive! Let's get her down. Hugo grab her legs!" Jesse shouted, excited about finding someone still alive after seeing so many dead. "Kat, check the others." Jesse and Hugo got the woman, Marcy Mayfield, down and laid her on the ceiling. Jesse looked her over, saw she had a leg fracture and a scrape where a pine branch penetrated the cabin and jabbed her in her the right shin. "Her leg is broken. We're going to have to splint it. How are the others, Kat?"

"I got one! He's alive, but he is bleeding out of his head. We've got to get him down," Kat said, as she reached up and unlatched the seat belt. The injured man, fell on top of Kat, knocking her and Ginger to the floor. Kat quickly wiggled out from under him and proceeded to check him over for other injuries. Kat checked his wallet and read the name on his driver's license, "Tyrone Miller. Ginger, I need some bandages!"

"Check his pupils," Jesse said loudly to Kat and Ginger.

"Hugo, you got this?" Jesse asked, motioning toward the unfinished splint on Marcy.

"Yeah, I can do it. I've raised five children, and they all have had a broken bone or two," he answered back.

The others looked on from the open end of the cabin, taking it all in and not wanting to be in the way as the sun started to fall behind the trees. Jack and Jon lingered in the back, waiting for a chance to slip away.

"Now, let's go," Jon said, bumping Jack on the side of his arm. Jack and Jon slipped away toward the front end of the plane as the others tended to the injured. They emptied a carry-on bag and gathered all the food they could find in the front end of the fuselage. It was mostly peanuts, pretzels, and a few sandwiches that were left over from the flight meal. Jack grabbed up a bottle of Jack Daniels from the floor, and Jon slapped it out his hand. "I need you thinking straight." Jack drew back like he was going to punch Jon in the face. "Really, now you're going do this?" Jon complained.

Jack flipped his brother off and picked up the Jack Daniels bottle, unscrewed the lid, and took a big swig. He dropped the bottle and gathered up several water bottles and stuffed them into another carryon bag he had emptied. As Jack maneuvered his way back out, he passed the U.S. marshal that sat next to Jesse and saw the shrapnel protruding from his face, and he said, "You got yours, Mr. Marshal Man." Then Jack and Jon disappeared into the woods.

# Chapter 3

"Dan! Dan! Where are you, Dan?" Marcy shouted as soon as she woke up. Marcy jerked her head around and tried to get a handle on where she was. She quickly realized that she was in a plane crash and was looking at seats above her. There were several people strapped in near her and their arms dangled down from the floor. She saw Dan's arms dangling and began to shout Dan's name again. "Dan! Dan!" She saw Hugo and screamed, "Get my husband down! Dan, we're coming!" She was frantic about getting to her husband. She tried to stand but fell back, and Hugo tried to catch her.

"Ma'am! Ma'am, he's gone," Hugo yelled, as he grabbed her by the shoulders and made her look at him. Tears formed in her eyes, and she began to sob.

"Are you sure? He might have been knocked out like me. Please check again," she insisted.

By that time, Jesse moved over to help Hugo and said, "We're sure, ma'am. We'll get Dan down for you, but first we need to get you out of here." Hugo and Jesse carried Marcy out of the cabin and sat her several yards away. They brought out Dan's body and laid him down next to her. She threw herself over Dan's shoulders and sobbed even louder as she shook him, hoping he would wake. Jesse and Hugo went back in and carried out Tyrone and laid him a few feet away from Marcy. Everyone was out and stood looking at Marcy weep over her dead husband.

The horrific day had finally sunk into everyone, and Kat began to cry. Shu had a wide-eyed look on her face like she'd just spaced out to turn the emotion off, and Hugo pulled her into an embrace. Jesse squatted down as he started to tear up but quickly wiped the unfallen tears away. Reverend Tucker knelt down beside Dan's body, waiting to console Marcy when her sobs slowed, and Ginger was leaned up against the fuselage with her face in her hands. Larry was picking through the debris on the ground in search of something, ignoring what was going on around him.

About a half hour had passed, and Jesse noticed that Jack and Jon were nowhere in sight. He stood up and walked over to Kat. "Have you seen Jack or Jon?" he asked.

"No, not for a while now, but I was busy and not paying attention to them," Kat answered. "Do you think Tyrone will wake up?"

"I don't know; one of his pupils is dilated, and he may have some brain swelling. We're just going to have to wait and see," Jesse explained. He walked over to Ginger and asked, "Did you see where Jack and Jon went; I don't see them anywhere?

"No, I didn't. They might be up at the other half of the cabin," she answered.

Jesse said, "Listen up, guys. We need to start preparing for the night. The temperature is dropping, and the sun is going down. We are going to lose any light we have so we need to build a fire and find a flashlight, and also figure out where we're going to bed down for the night. We need to get some blankets or some clothing to cover up with, but first we need to cover the injured."

"I thought Ginger was in charge?" Larry spouted out from a distance.

"We are in agreement on this," Ginger responded back quickly, as she stepped forward.

"We only have about twenty minutes, give or take, and it's going be pitch dark out here. So, we need to move fast. Let's gather up some luggage to search for flashlights, food, and blankets. Check the tags and if you find yours or one of ours, hang on to it; and if anyone finds mine please let me know. The tag will read *Jesse Gibson*," Jesse instructed.

"I'm not sure we can search other people's luggage, Jesse," Ginger asserted.

"Ginger, I know a lot of them will be locked or secured, but there are several around that have busted open. We still have a lot of carryon bags in the other half," Jesse responded.

"That's not what I meant. They're not our belongings," she added.

"Well, let's vote on it. There is no one here to rescue us, and we're not sure how long it will be. We can't call anyone, because all our phones are dead, and if the black box isn't working, we might be here for days. We don't have anywhere to get out of the cold other than the plane halves, with the dead, I might add. We have an immediate need of these things for survival, and we're not going to keep the items, other than the food since its consumable. But we might have to break into some luggage, and I'm sure the airline will reimburse who ever for their lost items in this crash. Don't you all think?" Jesse pressed. "Besides, once the plane hit the ground everything became evidence in an investigation."

"Yeah, I'm with Jesse," Larry chimed in. "These people will never get their stuff back."

"That's right, let's use all we can. I hope we're not here very long, but you never know," Hugo added.

"Kat, you agree with them?" Ginger asked.

"Yes, I do," she responded. "But what does the reverend have to say on the matter?"

"Please, everyone call me, Henry. In life or death situations, we have to make tough decisions. I believe it would be a worse crime for us to starve and freeze to death. My vote is to use whatever is here for our survival, since we've lost so much already," Reverend Tucker suggested.

"Okay, let's do it," Ginger declared.

"Let's just pile them up over here, and we can sort through them a couple at a time," Jesse motioned to a place by a big pine tree near Marcy and Dan's body. "We need to go to the front half to collect whatever food and water that's left, and we need to gather some fire wood."

"Kat, would you help me gather some wood?" Jesse asked.

"Sure," she responded.

Kat and Jesse slipped into the woods as the light was beginning to fade. Jesse reached down and picked up some dead branches and asked, "Are you okay?"

Kat, also reaching down to collect some branches, replied, "Yeah, but it's hard you know. So much destruction, and so much death, it makes you think. Why did I make it? Why was I spared? I feel so bad for Marcy and the families that don't even know yet."

"I know what you mean. I almost lost it watching Marcy mourn over her husband. I don't know any of these people, but seeing all the death breaks my heart. They are people loved by someone," he added. Making several trips in and out of the tree line, Kat and Jesse gathered a decent pile of wood to burn through the night. By then it had gotten dark, and Hugo was at work building a fire several feet away from Tyrone and Marcy.

Shu found a blanket and covered up Tyrone. While she did that, she noticed Marcy had laid her head on Dan's chest and was still crying. The others had about fourteen bags piled up and were starting to go through them by the fire light. Each person would read the owner's tag out loud before opening their bag.

"First one," Larry announced, as he twisted off the mini lock that was on it. "Todd Smith," he read. He unzipped it and flipped the lid open and right on top was a Busty Babes magazine. He grabbed it, opened it to the centerfold, dropped it open, and said, "Oh, would you look at that! Those are some nice…" Everyone grumbled at him to put that away. "Okay, Okay. I'll keep that for later."

Everybody just shook their heads at Larry as most retrieved a bag to pilfer through. Marcy continued to cry, and Shu just stared into the fire.

"I got a flash light, and it works. No, I got two flashlights that work," Hugo called out, as he shone the lights around the wreckage.

"Good, now we can go use the bathroom with a light," Shu spoke up, as she started to watch people dig in the luggage. "I have to go."

Hugo stood up and handed a flashlight to Shu and said, "I'll go with you."

Kat tossed Shu a half roll of toilet paper she'd found and added, "You might need this."

"Can I borrow one of those, we need to go the front half and gather any water and food," Jesse asked.

"Sounds good," Hugo replied and handed Jesse the other flashlight.

"I found a fruitcake and some fudge. It's all sliced up and ready in Tupperware. Must be Grandma's bag," Ginger spouted off before thinking and getting caught up in the moment.

"I'll have some of that. I'm starving," Larry declared.

Ginger tossed Larry the fruitcake; he tore into it and inhaled a piece, grabbed another, and passed it on. Ginger had found two water bottles in the tail that they all sipped on. Everyone had their fill of cake and fudge as they collected the necessary items they'd discussed. They had gathered together several blankets, jackets, towels, a few more flashlights, and some chips. Since it was December 15th and so close to Christmas, they found a large summer sausage gift pack, a tin of butter cookies, and several packs of candy canes. One whole bag contained wrapped

Christmas gifts, which they all agreed not to open any of them, at least not yet.

"Kat, Ginger, you two want to help me gather some food and water from the front half?" Jesse asked. All three of them walked to the front half of the fuselage and entered using a flashlight. "Please guys, be careful. Let's get all the water, food, and anything we'll need for the night. We can come back in the morning to get the rest."

"There's only four bottles of water and two packs of peanuts," Ginger fretted after looking around.

"That's it?" Kat protested.

"That's all I can see. There may be some scattered under seats, but yeah. That's it," Ginger repeated. "There's a bottle of Jack Daniels though."

"Jack and Jon Lucas," Jesse fumed. "They took it all and left us. I knew those guys were trouble."

"What do you mean?" Kat asked.

"They are fugitives now. They were being transported by this airline under the U.S. Marshal's office. I was sitting by a marshal during the crash. Ginger and I decided to keep it from the group until necessary," Jesse explained.

"I think we should tell the others," Kat asserted.

"I do too, now," Jesse agreed.

"They weren't handcuffed?" Kat asked.

"No, they had on shock vests. If they were to run or try something the marshals could shock them, kind of like a stun gun," Ginger explained.

"I never heard of those," Kat responded.

"Me either until today, but I bet they're not wearing them now," Ginger replied.

"Let's head back and inform the others," Jesse finalized. "Oh, the marshal gave me this card right before the crash and told me if he didn't make it to contact the name on it. Do you recognize the name, Ginger?" He shined the light on the card and held it up so Ginger and Kat could both read it.

"That's the name of the other marshal that was on board," Ginger announced.

"We didn't find anyone else alive, I don't know who it could be," Jesse wondered.

"I'm pretty sure; I don't think I've seen him since the crash. But I did see Jon and Jack check a few bodies, but they never called out," Ginger declared.

"We should try locating him tomorrow. I'm sure he has a pistol, and we can't have Jack or Jon getting a hold of it. I've got the other marshal's, just in case," Jesse admitted. "Grab that Jack Daniels, we can use it to disinfect or for a pain killer."

They headed back to the others and on arrival they saw that Marcy had cried herself to sleep upon Dan's chest. Tyrone was still unconscious and covered. Everyone else was sitting by the fire either piddling with something they'd found or just staring into the flames. "Hey guys, listen. Jack and Jon are criminals and were being transported to Atlanta for drug trafficking and car theft. They are the two guys that were here earlier and are now gone. The two marshals that were with them are dead. They might be armed and dangerous now, plus they took all the food and most of the water and took off. We only have four bottles and two packs of peanuts," Jesse informed. "We should probably have lookouts throughout the night. We don't know what they're capable of; plus, we need to keep this fire going for rescue planes or choppers. Jesse glanced at his old wind-up Timex, "It's about 8:30 now, and we'll start watch at 9:30. I'll take first watch and then wake Hugo and Shu in three hours."

"I'll watch with you," Kat quickly spoke up.

"Okay, Rev—I mean Henry—you and Ginger next, then Larry and I will finish out the night," Jesse added.

"That's alright, Jesse; once I'm up, I'm up. Old guys don't sleep that much anyway. I'll finish the night with you. Larry, you're off the hook," Henry petitioned.

"Alright, but I was hoping to watch Ginger. I mean, watch with Ginger," Larry responded, winking at Ginger. She gave Larry a mean look but didn't say anything as everyone else just ignored what he said.

"We'll search for water in the morning. But for now, I heard there was summer sausage and butter cookies," Jesse requested. He settled down by the fire and started to munch on some sausage.

"Why do you all think help hasn't come yet?" Henry asked the group.

"I don't know," Kat responded.

"We might have been off course, or maybe the black box was damaged, and they are searching but haven't found us yet," Jesse added. "By my best guess, we are somewhere in the Appalachian Mountains, and it's a big place. We were about half way through the flight. We could be in any of about three or four states."

"Are there bears out here?" Hugo asked, concerned.

"Yes, there are black bears. They usually won't bother people, but we do have a lot of dead bodies lying around. We might want to watch out for coyotes though. That's another reason we should watch through the night. The animals will smell the blood and be coming for a closer look. So you guys on watch stay alert," Jesse answered.

"What about bigfoot and chupacabras?" Larry teased.

"Seriously people, do I need to be worried about something eating me in the night?" Ginger fretted.

"No, the animals are as afraid of us as we are of them. Whoever is on watch will keep you safe, but be careful when you use the bathroom. I don't believe there's such a thing as a big foot or a chupacabra," Jesse assured.

# Chapter 4

The crackling of the burning wood filled their ears as everyone settled down by the fire. Their shadows danced on the broken plane and the trees around them as the red and orange embers floated into the night sky. They were silent for several minutes as they thought through the past events of the day. They munched on the chips and snacks they'd found, and Jesse checked on Tyrone and Marcy. Once he was finished, he took a seat among them and sucked on a candy cane.

"How did you know to do all you did today? Helping the injured, I mean," Hugo directed his question to Jesse.

"I was a paramedic for a couple of years, ages ago; I was also a combat medic in Iraq for the Army," Jesse replied.

"Thank you for your service, but what do you do now, and were you flying home or going somewhere?" Hugo asked.

Jesse nodded and replied, "I go every year to Niagara River for steelhead fishing and meet up with my old high school buddies there. You can catch some big steelhead this time of year. As far as what I do, my dad died last year and left me his estate that I've been selling off for the past year. But before that, I was a carpenter for ten years. How about you?"

"I'm the owner of several auto parts stores in Texas called Longhorn Auto Parts. Shu is my secretary and my mistress," Hugo declared and giggled, reaching over to hold Shu's hand.

"Yes, it's true. We run the stores together and go on these trips to meet our parts suppliers, but they're just our cover. Hugo is married with five children and three grandchildren, and we are like one big family. His children call me Aunty Shu, but I don't think anyone knows about us. At least no one has said anything," Shu spoke up, shocking the group. "I've been with Hugo since he started twenty years ago. Remember Hugo, when my parents and I moved from Taipei?"

"Oh yes, I remember it well," Hugo responded. "She had just come from China, and I had never seen a more beautiful and mysterious woman. I asked her to work for me soon after meeting her. I was already married with two kids, and I knew if she worked for me, I could see her all the time. I didn't even care if she knew anything about business or auto parts, but as it turned out she had a BA in business. We made a great team, still do."

"He pays me well. And we are very lucky to be alive together today," Shu declared, as she turned and kissed Hugo on the lips.

"What about you, Kat?" Shu asked.

"I guess we're going around the fire. What else do we have to do, right? Well, I'm a ghost writer. I write articles, short stories, and sometimes speeches; things like that for people who get all the credit, but I make a decent living at it. I was visiting my sister in New York. She just had a baby and made me an aunt for the second time. A boy, Lucas James Scott," Kat replied. Several of the group congratulated her on her new nephew.

It was silent for about a minute or two then Ginger said, "I'm a flight attendant." Everyone looked at her for a second and then laughed a little. "This was my first flight as most of you already know. I just wanted to see more of the world and thought it would be a good way to do that. But I think I'll never get on a plane again. I'm going to have to re-think my future."

"Well sweetie, you're not alone. I just lost the biggest deal of my life. I'm bankrupt by now. Maybe I can sue the airline," Larry whined. "I put everything I had into this one property, and I was flying to the closing that was this evening. Now the bank has repossessed it, because I was so behind. They gave me until 7 pm to come up with a payment. It was a $750,000 balloon. I'm broke, completely broke, and now I'm homeless since they took my apartment."

"What was the property?" Henry asked.

"It was an apartment building I'd bought and had remodeled and I was living there. It had taken too long and squeezed me dry. I had a buyer, but with this crash the time ran out," Larry explained.

"I'll pray for you; I'll pray for all of you," Henry declared.

"Thanks Henry, sounds like we all need it," Jesse admitted.

"Yeah right, like that's going help. Thanks anyway, Henry, but I'll do for myself. Your prayers didn't keep this plane in the air, did it?" Larry protested. Henry didn't defend himself, and no one else spoke up.

"What's your story, Henry?" Hugo asked, breaking the awkwardness.

"I have been a preacher for fifty years and pastored the same church for the last thirty-five of those years. I was thinking of retiring and was on my way home from a pastor's retreat at Niagara Falls before I told my church in Jackson, Georgia. My wife is seventy-two and I'm sixty-eight; we think it's about time. We want to do a little traveling and focus more on our grandchildren and family," Henry responded.

"Hey! Look at that, "Larry exclaimed, pointing up at the sky. Everyone looked up and saw red, green, and orange lights dancing in the distant star-scattered sky. It moved across the night and covered the darkness as far as the eye could see. It illuminated the land enough for everyone to see well. It lasted for about twenty-five minutes as the group laid back and took in the show.

"What do you think is happening?" Kat questioned.

"It's the northern lights," Larry answered back.

"Yeah, except we're in the south. Must be some kind of electrical storm," Jesse declared.

"It's beautiful," Ginger beamed.

"Yes, it is," Shu agreed.

They laid there in silence and amazement for the rest of the light show and soon watched it disappear from the night sky. Henry had fallen asleep, and everyone else continued to lay there trying to go to sleep. Jesse got up and whispered to Kat to follow, "It's time for our watch."

Jesse handed Kat a flashlight and said, "Let's do a perimeter walk, keeping our eyes out for predators of any kind." Kat stayed close to Jesse as they made their way around the crash scene, looking for anything that moved, pausing for minutes at a time to observe the areas.

"Are you married?" Kat asked out of the blue.

"Widowed for about four years now," Jesse spoke in low tone, trying to not wake the others.

"Oh, I'm sorry," she said.

"It's okay, you couldn't have known. Manda and I were married for seventeen years. Amanda was her name; I called her Manda. We have two kids, Jacob who is twenty-one and Paige who is eighteen," he revealed. "What about you?"

"I'm single, never married. I came close once, but he cheated on me. I only have a cat named Leaf. I live in a high-rise apartment in Atlanta, but I grew up on a farm in South Georgia. Where are your kids?"

"Jacob is in Germany in the Army, and Paige is on a Christmas vacation with her boyfriend's family in Florida. Why the name Leaf?"

"She has a spot on her side that looks just like an oak leaf. I've had her since she was a kitten. She's about eight now. My dad got her for me when I moved out to keep me company, I guess. Have you dated since...you know?"

"After about three years, my kids and family kept telling me to get back out there. I dated a few times, but that's about it. I've been too busy with my daughter and getting her ready to go off to college, and also handling my Dad's estate. Are you active in the dating game?"

"No, I go out every once in a blue moon, but it's usually with friends. I haven't found anyone that interesting. What was your wife like?"

"Well, she was very beautiful. She had blond hair and the deepest blue eyes I'd ever seen. She was thin and petite, a little like you but she could hold her own. Tough, you know. A terrific mother and a perfect wife, but she had her flaws. One day I came home from work, and she had decided she was going to remodel the bathroom. She had gotten my sledge hammer and started to hammer away at the tile wall and busted straight through to the living room. When she got an idea in her head, she wasn't going to stop until she made it happen, which usually meant me fixing it for her." Jesse took a long pause as tears watered his eyes. "We were so in love. We were high school sweethearts, and every day with her...felt like we'd just fallen in love." He sniffed and rubbed his nose and said, "Sorry."

"You have nothing to be sorry about. Sounds like she and I might've been friends if I'd known her," Kat smiled. "What happened if you don't mind me asking?"

"It was the strangest thing. She came home from the grocery store on a Tuesday after picking up dinner, and it had been raining that day. She slipped and hit her head on the steps but shook it off and continued to go about her day. She forgot to tell me, or she just didn't want to tell me because I was always ragging her about some slick shoes she wore all the time. But later that night, she had a seizure, and I called an ambulance. The doctor said her brain was swelling, that she'd hit her head just right. I corrected him and told him she hit her head just wrong. She had several more seizures, and then she was gone. My kids and I had time to say goodbye though. The doctor told us she might not make it through the night. Right before her last seizure, we had about thirty minutes where she was completely coherent and clear-minded. I knew it wouldn't be long after that. I'd seen it in Iraq, clarity right before death. It was either fear or complete peace. Her last words were, 'Don't worry, my loves; heaven is a place of great joy and peace. I see Him; He is here with me.' She was always more religious than I was, but I know in my heart she was talking about the Lord. When she died, I was out of my mind for a couple of months, until I realized my kids still needed me. It got better as each day passed, but every once in while I forget she's gone."

Jesse and Kat swapped information about each other's lives, and when their watch was over, they woke up Hugo and Shu. Jesse stoked the fire and they both laid down and fell asleep.

# Chapter 5

"Jesse, Jesse, wake up," Henry shook Jesse awake.

"What is it? What's wrong?" Jesse rose up quickly.

"Nothing, it's just time for the last watch," Henry declared in a whisper.

"Okay, I'm up," Jesse announced also in a whisper. Jesse stoked the fire and added some wood for warmth. "Was there any issues through the night?"

"No, we did spot a coyote, but it ran after we shined a light on him. I thought Ginger was going to squeeze my arm off when she spotted him. She reminded me of my oldest granddaughter Bianca; whenever she would get scared, she would always cling to me and squeeze my arm," Henry added.

"When did you last walk the perimeter?" Jesse asked.

"About an hour ago," he answered.

"Ready to do it again?" Jesse and Henry walked the perimeter, shining their flashlights all around. It was the same as with Kat; they would walk several yards looking all around and stop to focus on their surroundings. They spotted a coyote gnawing on the arm of a dead passenger. "There, look at that. We're going to have to do something with these bodies if help doesn't get here soon or move camp further into the woods," Jesse remarked.

Henry picked up a hand-sized rock and hurled it at the animal. He missed, but the coyote ducked a little and then went back to gnawing on the arm. He picked up another and threw it and hit the coyote's side. The animal yelped and ran off into the woods. "Git!" Henry hollered. He quickly looked back at the fire where everyone was sleeping to make sure no one woke.

"It's okay, I think your voice carried down the hill instead of up to them," Jesse reassured. "Let's continue; his mate may be around here also." The time passed slowly for the two of them waiting for the sun to rise. They shone their lights into the woods and spotted a few more pieces of luggage that they could retrieve at daylight.

"I think we should have some kind of service for the dead, especially for Marcy. I'm not sure how she's going be in the morning. She's distraught with grief. Maybe it will bring her some comfort or closure," Henry suggested, as they stood together looking at the luggage. "I'm not sure if she's up for that, but I can ask her."

"I think that's one of my suitcases. I have no problem with that if everyone else is okay with it, but we need to address our water issue first, and we should decide what to do about the bodies," Jesse responded.

"Of course, survival first, then we can address the spiritual needs," Henry agreed. "But for Marcy, survival is foreign to her right now as her loss is surreal."

"I can relate to her loss in more ways than one, and I do sympathize. We'll bring it up when everyone wakes up," Jesse added.

The morning light crept over the trees as the mass wreckage came into view, and the survivors lay nestled under blankets, clothes, and towels by the fire. Tyrone sat straight up and began to scream, "Mamma! Mamma! They're coming for me! Mamma!"

Henry and Jesse rushed over to him, and he had a terrified look on his face. He stared straight at them but didn't seem to really see them. His left pupil was still dilated, and Jesse grabbed his shoulders and said, "Sir, can you hear me?" Jesse waved his hand in front of Tyrone's face with no response. "He's blind, and I think he's hallucinating."

Everyone was startled awake by the screams and was either sitting up or standing, watching, even Marcy sat up and watched. Tyrone went into a convulsion and then slumped forward as Jesse laid him down on his side. "He's dead," Jesse declared. Jesse stood up quickly, as emotions began to wash over him. He turned and hurried away to compose himself.

Everyone looked at each other and Kat said quietly, "That's how his wife died, a head injury." Everyone was silent as they began to stretch and ponder what the day would bring them, and if they would get to go home soon.

"What do you think he was screaming about? You think his mom was on the plane?" Shu asked everyone.

"He boarded the plane alone and sat next to strangers as far as I could tell," Ginger answered. "Maybe he was in some kind of trouble."

"We'll never know," Hugo added.

"Maybe it was who he saw as he was dying," Henry offered, as he closed the man's eyes.

"What, the Boogieman? Come on, Preacher, we're not your Sunday morning congregation. Stop with the scare tactics," Larry objected.

"Larry, have you ever seen the movie *Ghost* with Patrick Swayze and Demi Moore?" Henry asked.

"Yeah, when I was twelve. I was young when that movie came out," Larry retorted.

"Okay, remember the black ghost-like creatures that came and took Willie and Carl away when they died?" Henry reasoned.

"Oh yeah, I remember that. I couldn't sleep for days after I saw that movie," Kat interjected. "I was just a kid."

Henry nodded and said, "That's all I'm saying."

Larry didn't say anything after that, and Jesse returned after several minutes and declared, "We need to find water, like now. We also need to have a look at where we are, and if something is close enough to us to get help. Maybe there's a town, a house, something nearby."

"Let's split up and walk in all four directions for a certain distance. Then return to report what we saw or found," Hugo asserted.

"Yeah, let's do that," Larry chimed in.

"But let's go in pairs for safety's sake," Jesse cautioned.

"I'll stay here with Marcy," Henry offered.

"Good, that'll work. Hugo, you and Shu go east, toward the sun. Kat, you and I will go south. Larry, you and Ginger go west, away from the sun. When we get back, we'll go north I guess, if we don't find anything. Try to walk in a straight line, so you don't lose your way back," Jesse instructed.

"Sounds like a plan," Shu added.

"Ginger, you okay going with Larry?" Jesse asked.

"I can handle guys like him," she answered.

Larry looked at them with his hands wide open and objected, "Guys like me..."

Jesse ignored Larry. "Let's all take something to fill with water. Walk for about twenty to thirty minutes and if you find water, bring some back. If you find a house or a town, come back to tell us before going forward. We'll all go together."

"Take something to eat with you for energy. We still have some summer sausage and butter cookies," Kat suggested.

Jesse grabbed Larry's skinny arm and leaned in to whisper, "If you try anything with Ginger, you'll have me to answer to."

Larry threw up his hands and said, "Whoa, don't worry, Doc. I'll be a gentleman."

"You better be," Jesse asserted.

"Let's do this," Hugo coaxed.

They all wandered around the crash site to find something to carry water in. Ginger grabbed two empty water bottles from last night to take. Hugo and Shu took an almost-empty liquor bottle, and each took the last two swallows. Kat and Jesse took the fudge container and poured the bottle of Jack Daniels out into it and took the bottle for water. They all met back by the fire.

Jesse and Kat retrieved the three suitcases from the woods and stacked two of them on top of the suitcase full of Christmas gifts. He unlocked his and flung it open. He took out an 8" Bowie Case knife, a Swiss Army knife, a Leatherman multitool, and a 6" fish fillet knife. He handed the Leatherman to Henry and said, "Just in case." He handed the fillet knife to Hugo and the Swiss Army knife to Ginger and then strapped the bowie knife to his belt.

"You came prepared, huh, Doc," Larry questioned.

"I was in the woods steelhead fishing, so yeah, I did," Jesse replied. "We did see a coyote gnawing on a body last night, and the bears may not have all gone into hibernation yet. So be watchful and careful. Let's go." Jesse bent down, zipped his suitcase, and locked it. They all walked into woods in their designated directions.

# Chapter 6

Larry and Ginger had been walking through the woods in silence for about five minutes. Ginger was in front of Larry, and he said, "Everything looks good from here."

Ginger stopped and turned to face him and said, "Larry, why are you so creepy? Why must you say things like that to me or any woman? It doesn't help your situation at all. We find it offensive and pervy."

"Just admiring the view, Honey, don't get your panties in a bunch," he cautioned.

"Agh!" she grunted and shook her head at him. She turned and started walking again.

They were heading in a downward direction, and the walk back was going be a chore for them. It would be especially for Ginger since her shoes were not made for the woods, but luckily the airline allowed their flight attendants to wear slacks in the winter. They began walking through some thicker brush, and Ginger forcefully pushed her way through. She caught her foot on a vine and tripped, rolling down a steep hill and over the side of a high drop off to a river. She barely caught herself on a thick tree root and was hanging on about fifteen feet above whitewater rapids. "Larry!" she called out.

Larry sprang into action and dove to grab her hands and began to pull her up. He heaved and strained to get her up, and he fell back, pulling her on top of him. She laid her head on his chest, and Larry started to say something. "Well…"

"Don't. Don't ruin the moment with a pervy comment," she said, raising her head and looking at him. "Thank you."

"I was only going to say, I guess you found water." They both started laughing, as she rolled off of him.

"Oh no, the bottles!" she exclaimed.

"I think you dropped them when you tripped up the hill. Let's grab them and find an easier way down to the river."

They both stood up and slowly climbed up the hill, pulling on saplings and vines to aid them. They searched for an easier way to reach the river's edge and get some much-needed water. As they found a calmer and gentler flowing area, Ginger asked, "Do you think we can drink some? It's mountain water, right?"

"I wouldn't drink any unless you want to get the runs. We should boil it first, I think. I'm sure the Doc will know all about it."

"I'm so thirsty. I want to drink some," she admitted.

"I wouldn't."

"I won't, but I'm really thirsty." Ginger filled a bottle and handed it to Larry and then filled the other. "Wow, it's really pretty here, and the sound of the water flowing is peaceful."

"The view's not bad either."

"Stop."

"No, really. You are very pretty, and you here, by the river, it's very scenic. Picture-perfect almost," he praised.

"Well, thank you. You're not so bad looking either, Mr. Larry. What is your last name?"

"It's Larry Wright, and yours?"

"Ginger Green, my family and friends call me G because my middle name is Gale. Ginger Gale Green, it's very nice to meet you Larry Wright."

"Likewise, G. May I call you G?"

"You may. Let's sit a minute to rest up for the uphill walk back." They both sat down on a large rock overlooking the river. Larry picked up a small rock and tossed it into the river.

"It's a defense mechanism, my *perviness,* as you called it. I always had a hard time talking to girls, and I thought I met the one I was going to love forever. We got married, and I thought we were happy. After about a year, I came home from work one day and found her in our bed with my neighbor. So, it took me a long time to get over her, and I guess I have some trust issues with women. I don't trust any, or anyone, really. My neighbor was a good friend of mine."

"I'm so sorry, Larry. I could never do that to someone; I'm a very loyal person. My dad said it is one of my weaknesses. I always had a hard time breaking it off with guys even when I knew I should. I'm too trusting."

"Did I sense that maybe you are interested in me, or did I read that all wrong?"

"You did save my life, we did survive a major plane crash, and I said you were cute. And I like the way your sandy blond hair is sticking up everywhere, and your eyes… They are, well, I can see a beautiful man in there. So yeah, you're Spidey senses are correct." She bent over and kissed him on his cheek. "You don't have to trust me yet. We can take it slow and see how it goes." Larry blushed and tried to slick down his messed up hair. "Don't, let it go. It looks great like that, and I like it."

Larry smiled and put his hands down, "I've never dated a redhead before."

"Aren't you in for a treat," she replied as they both giggled at each other. Let's head back, I'm still so thirsty."

"Wait, shouldn't this place here…" Larry stretched out his arms and motioned all around them. "Be the place of our first kiss?"

"You are a romantic, I knew it." Ginger leaned into him and their lips touched, and he pressed his firmly against hers. The kiss lasted for several seconds, and they pulled apart. "Wow! That was very nice, Larry."

"Yes, it was. Thank you."

"For what?"

"For getting through to me. I needed that." They started to walk back to camp holding hands.

# Chapter 7

Hugo and Shu walked straight with the sun in their faces, as it flickered through the bare tree branches. *Crunch, crunch, crunch* was the sound they heard with each step they took deeper into the woods. A breeze blew the tops of the trees, and they swayed back and forth, causing their limbs to rub together and make some squeaking and clicking noises. Hugo stopped and faced Shu. "You are still so lovely in the morning light," he said.

Shu stepped up to him and hugged him and then kissed him on the cheek. "I'm so thankful, Hugo; we made it through the crash. We're still alive. Maria must be worried sick about you."

"I know, I wish I could call her and let her know we are okay."

"I had a great time this past week, but when we get back to Texas..." Shu dropped her head and said, "I'm so ashamed, Hugo, to be doing this to Maria. We were spared in this crash for some strange reason. What random order of things that we would live and not all those others. I love you so much, but I can't be your mistress any longer."

"I know you're shaken up over the crash, but we've been together like this forever," he responded. "Why the sudden change?"

"It was hearing myself talk about us. It's not right, and it's especially not right for your wife and family. I saw the look on everyone's faces last night."

"Shu, darling, Maria knows about us. She's okay with us."

"What! Maria *knows*? I can never face her again. How long has she known?"

"For many years now."

"Oh no, why didn't you tell me? She still hugs me and kisses my cheek when she sees me; we exchange Christmas gifts. I think

I'm going to be sick." Shu bent over and held her stomach and then dropped down to her knees.

Hugo got down on his knees beside her and began to rub her back. "I didn't tell you because of this. Maria knows you make me happy. That's why she loves you. We can go on like this conversation never happened. You've had these guilty episodes before."

"No, we can't; it's different now. I've spent my whole life being a man's mistress," Shu spoke as if she were speaking to herself.

"It's not different! Maria is okay with it, with us, together," he declared.

"Hugo, Maria is one of my closest friends, and I'm her husband's concubine. We were spared for a reason, and I'm not going to keep hurting my friend. I love you, Hugo, but this, us, is over. I quit!"

"You're choosing my wife over me? Ay, caramba!" He exclaimed in his native tongue. "Are you kidding me? Come on, Shu, I'll give you time off. I need you for the business and for me. I love you, and I'll give you some space if that's what you want."

"Do you hear that?" she asked.

"What?"

"Shhh, listen." They both froze and listened intently. "It's a voice, it's saying… Help! It's coming from that direction," she pointed northeast. "Do you hear it?"

"Yeah, I do. Let's go check it out," he suggested. They both got up and trotted in the direction they thought they heard the voice coming from. They stopped and listened. "Hello!" Hugo called out.

"Hey! Up here!" the voice sounded on top of them.

They both looked up and scanned the trees but didn't see anything. "Here!" the voice called again. They looked to their right, and way up a giant sycamore tree, an airplane seat was wedged between a couple of large limbs. There were two people strapped into the seat and the one that spoke sat on the outer edge of the seat that counter levered out away from the trunk.

"Can you help me; can you get me down?" a boy called down from the wedged seat. "I'm afraid to unbuckle. If I do, I will fall."

"What about the person next to you?" Shu called up.

"His head has been cut off, and it's just a dead body beside me," the boy responded.

"We need to go get the others; maybe the'll know what to do. We definitely need more help," Hugo suggested.

"I'll stay here and talk to him; you go back and get someone," Shu responded.

"I'm going to get some help to get you down," Hugo called up to the boy. "She is going to stay here with you. Her name is Shu, what's yours?"

"Austin!" he called down.

"Okay, Austin, I'll back in a few minutes," Hugo announced and then turned to Shu. "I'll be back as quick as I can, and we'll finish our conversation later." Shu nodded and Hugo took off back to their camp site.

# Chapter 8

Kat and Jesse walked south in the same direction that the plane's fuselage pointed. The pines stopped where they had crashed, and the woods opened up into big hardwood trees. Several squirrels scurried away, and one jumped up on a tree trunk and began to bark and flick his tail to alert other squirrels of danger. Small patches of snow glistened in the sunlight on the forest floor. "Look, a pecan tree," Kat declared. "There are still quite a few pecans here on the ground. Looks like there are a couple of pecan trees here."

"We'll gather some on our way back, but we might have to fight the squirrels to get some," Jesse said, pointing to the barking squirrel.

"We had several pecan trees back on the farm. I used to love gathering them up with my dad and then cracking them all with my mom. She would make the best pecan pies," she revealed, as they continued walking. "Mom won the blue ribbon several years in row with her pecan pie in the Jingle Jangle Christmas cook-off in Wilcox County."

He smiled at her and repeated, "Jingle Jangle Christmas cook-off. That must have been something."

She smiled back and said, "It was, and the food was great. It was a simpler time back then. It was a wonder I didn't turn out to be a fat kid."

"Well, you lived on a farm and you had plenty of chores, right?"

"Yes, I did."

"You must've worked it off."

"I guess so. I always played hard too, running, climbing, and pushing my Barbie van around."

"Yeah, I had my GI Joe jeep and a mountain of dirt to get filthy in, made my mom proud."

"Really, my Barbie married a GI Joe. They're still together to this day," Kat joked. "In a box in my dad's attic."

"What happened to Ken?"

"Ken wasn't man enough for my Barbie," she declared.

They laughed and walked for a few minutes, pondering their childhood memories. Jesse wondered if Paige had heard the news about his plane crashing yet, if even Jacob had heard. Kat wondered what Jesse was thinking about as they walked. They came to a ledge that inclined downward for several yards before leveling off and declining downward again. They looked out over the ledge and saw nothing but treetops that rose and fell like waves in an ocean photograph, no roads, no homes, and no towns. "Let's head back and gather some of those pecans and see if anyone else found anything," he suggested.

"Can we sit a minute or two before we go back?" she asked.

"Sure, we can sit and admire the view. We've only been walking for about ten minutes," he motioned for her to sit.

"Are you always this put-together? I mean, a man with a plan?" she asked.

"No, but I think I'm a survivor, so I'm always thinking of my next move before I have to make it. How about you? You seem okay, considering what you've just gone through."

"I'm a survivor also, but I like to watch things play out. People, I mean. Being a writer, people-watching is a favorite past time of mine. I've been watching *you*, Jesse Gibson."

Jesse smiled a little and said, "Well, do you like what you see?"

"So far, so good."

"I aim to please."

"Is that right?"

"Yes, ma'am."

Kat began to shiver, and he scooted closer to her and put his arm around her. He began to rub her shoulder to create friction for heat. "I'm not making a move; I'm just trying to warm you up. It's cold out here."

"Um-hum," she hummed and laid her head on his shoulder, and they both gazed out over the view.

About a minute passed and Jesse said, "You know I haven't seen or heard any other planes or choppers, have you? Even last night, I didn't see any plane lights, just those strange aurora borealis lights."

"I guess our moment is over. I haven't either."

"Sorry, I'm contemplating an explanation for our cell phones not working and the lights we saw last night."

"Yeah, you have a theory?" she asked.

"I do, but I'm not sure. I'm thinking a solar flare might have knocked out our cells and maybe even crashed the plane."

Kat pulled away and turned to face him, "You mean a sun storm caused us to crash?"

"Maybe, I'm just guessing, but it would explain a few things. Not necessarily a storm but a flare. It's a sudden explosion on the sun that projects magnetic energy, and we might have flown through it," he explained.

"Wow, what are chances of that?"

"It's just a theory. We better collect those pecans and check in," he suggested.

They began to walk back to camp, and Kat thought about Jesse's theory and what the others would think about it. She looked over at him and considered his brown Carhartt jacket like the one her dad used to wear. It reminded her of him. A lot about Jesse reminded her of her dad, a man that she loved and admired very much. She felt very comfortable and safe with Jesse and when she looked into his eyes, she felt herself being drawn to him. When they arrived at the pecan trees, they filled their pockets with pecans.

Jesse looked over at Kat while she was collecting some nuts. He thought of how attracted he was to her and how well she filled out her Levis. Of course he had noticed and even admired beautiful women, but Kat possessed a pulling or longing in him. He had never felt that kind of attraction to a woman other than his wife, Amanda. He was afraid of the attraction, afraid of forgetting Amanda. He wondered if it was possible to fall in love again and have what he had with Amanda, that kind of bond and closeness. Amanda was his best friend. What would his kids think of Kat? Would she like them? He thought these kinds of relationships are complicated and created too many variables. But he couldn't deny that he definitely had a connection with Kat; plus, she was very beautiful.

They both stood upright and looked at each other and felt guilty of their thoughts of one another. Kat smiled at him and asked, "Got enough?"

"My pockets are full, let's go." They both walked back into camp and saw Hugo burst out of the tree line without Shu.

# Chapter 9

Jon took in a long drag on his cigarette, bent down, and blew the smoke into Jack's face. Jack coughed a little and opened his eyes, "Where'd you get the smokes?"

"I took them off a stiff last night," Jon replied.

"Give me one," Jack demanded.

Jon dropped the pack of cigarettes on his chest with the lighter inserted in the clear lining of the pack. "You need to get up. We need to get moving. The FEDs could have the dogs on us by now," Jon urged.

"We walked most of the night; nah, I ain't heard no dogs."

"I spotted a shack a ways off we need to check out. Maybe they got a truck or something we can get moving faster in," Jon pondered.

"Alright, let me take a dump first."

Jack stepped away to do his business, and Jon pulled out the marshal's pistol, a P229 Sig Sauer .357 to check the ammo. He dropped the clip and saw it was full and checked the chamber and a round was already chambered. He slapped the clip back in, clicked the safety, and tucked the Sig into the back of his waistline. "Pinch it off! Let's go, Jack," he called.

Jack joined Jon as they walked toward the shack Jon had spotted. "What you think the deal was with those lights last night?" Jack asked.

"Don't know, never seen that before. Who knows, but it helped us make some good time," Jon answered.

Jack didn't respond; he opened a bag of peanuts and poured some into his mouth. The closer they got to the shack, they could see that it was better than just a shack, a cabin in fact, but a little disguised to look like a shack from far off. They noticed several fruit trees that bore no fruit since it was winter and a sizeable garden site that was tended regularly. Jon pointed to a four wheeler ATV under camo netting. It was draped over a carport-type structure along with a dirt bike and a canoe. Jon pulled out the Sig, clicked the safety off, and motioned to Jack to follow his lead as they approached the front door. Jack picked up a large stick that was on top of a pile of fire wood and held it in the ready position as they moved to both sides of the door. Jack reached for the door knob.

"That won't be necessary, Mister," a voice said from out of nowhere.

Jack and Jon looked all around. "Do you see anybody?" Jon whispered to Jack. Jack shook his head no and then reached for the door knob again.

"I said, don't!" the voice exclaimed, as a man stepped out from behind a pine tree about fifteen yards from them covered in a camo ghillie suit.

"What the…" Jon questioned.

"What do you want?" the man asked.

"We're U.S. Marshals looking for a fugitive that escaped custody," Jack explained, glancing over at Jon.

"Well, they're not here. Show me your badges," the man demanded.

"Sure, no problem," Jon said, nodding to Jack. Jon slung the pistol around and fired three shots at the man as Jack crashed through the man's cabin door. The man fired off a shot as he fell to the ground. His shot hit Jon in the back, as he followed Jack through the door. He slammed the door behind him and tumbled to the floor. "I'm hit! I'm shot. Shot bad." Jack went to his side as Jon lay on his back, blood pooling beneath him. "Jack, I'm not going to make it. Jack… Jack…" he went limp, and he was dead.

"Jon! Jon!" Jack shook him a little then checked for a pulse on his neck. "I'm sorry, bro." Jack grabbed the Sig and went to the door and peeked out to see where the man was. Jack saw him lying right where he had been standing. "You killed my brother, you nut sack!" He listened, but there was no response. He peeked out again and saw that the man wasn't moving. He checked the clip and chamber on the Sig for ammo and then slowly opened the door and approached the man with the pistol on point toward him. He saw the rifle the man used to kill his brother, and he kicked it away. He gave the body a swift kick in the side, but there was no movement. He bent down and rolled the guy over and saw blood all over the ground and on the camo strands. There were three bullet holes in the man's chest. "You always were a good shot," Jack said out loud to his brother.

# Chapter 10

The buzzards gained in number as they circled high above the crash site. The smell of death was heavy in the air, and the weight of so many losses was upon Henry's heart. He sat off from Marcy while he prayed for the families of those that lay dead and mangled around him. He began to weep and lament over the pain that the families would feel, and he pleaded with God to grant them peace. "Father, your ways are above my ways, and I don't understand why you allowed this to happen. But I know you are a loving God, and this did not escape your knowledge. I plead with you, Lord; grant the families of the deceased here peace and may your goodness pour out upon them in this time of grief. I know that all things work together for good for those who love you, and I ask that you would allow us to find our way home again, in Jesus' name, amen."

Henry finished praying and composed himself before walking over to Marcy to check on her. She was sitting at the fire with her back to Dan's body, staring at its mesmerizing, flickering flames and gently rubbing her broken leg. Henry sat down next to her and asked, "How are you?"

"I don't know what I'll do without him. I feel like someone shot me in the chest, but there's no physical wound. We were still newlyweds, only been married a year. We dated for three though. He was the love of my life; now he's gone. How can God be so cruel?" she said.

"I don't have an answer to your question, but suffering is a part of life. We partake in the sufferings of Christ. I know that doesn't bring you much comfort if any, but if we lose faith in God through the sufferings, the sufferings become useless. Was Dan a believer?"

"Yes, he was a very godly man, a deacon in our church," she answered, as tears ran down her face.

"Then you can have peace in the knowledge that he's with the Lord now."

"I do, but that doesn't make the hole go away."

"I know, I know," Henry said, as he put his arm around her to console her. She laid her head on his shoulder, and they sat in silence for a while.

"We need to wrap him up and secure his body. I don't want any animals getting to him," Marcy broke the silence and sat up to face Henry.

"Okay, I'll go look for something to wrap him in," he answered. He walked around the crash site in search of something to use. He wanted something that was big enough and maybe waterproof in case it rained before help arrived. He remembered he saw someone had a shower curtain in their suitcase. It wasn't in a package, and he wondered if someone had stolen it from a hotel. He retrieved it and a sheet from the same suitcase and spread them out next to Dan's body with the sheet on the bottom. Henry rolled his body on to the sheet and shower curtain then wrapped him up in them.

"We'll get a couple of the men to help carry his body into the tail to keep him safe," he suggested.

"That'll be good," she answered. "Here come Jesse and Kat."

Just then Hugo burst out of the woods and yelled, "Where's Jesse?"

Henry pointed to Jesse and Kat as they were walking toward them. "What's wrong?" Henry asked.

"We found a boy stuck high in a tree, and we need some help getting him down," Hugo explained.

Jesse and Kat walked up, and Jesse said, "You found what?"

"A boy high in a tree, he's stuck in his seat with a dead body next to him and is afraid to unbuckle because he'll fall," Hugo explained.

"What can we use to get him down?" Jesse asked everyone.

"Belts! Gather belts off the dead and strap them together," Marcy blurted out. Everyone looked at Marcy with surprise since she had been so uninvolved for so long. "It will work. Dan told me a story one time that he used belts buckled together to pull his brother out of a well, when he was a teenager," she said, urging them to move with her hands.

"Let's gather the belts," Kat encouraged.

They gathered several belts, and Henry said, "I'll stay here with Marcy."

"Make sure you elevate your leg. Is it hurting you?" Jesse asked Marcy.

"Yes, it's throbbing some," she answered.

"I may have to set it when I get back," Jesse observed.

"Won't that hurt?" Marcy asked with worry in her voice.

"Very much, but I'll be as gentle as I can. You might want to get started on some Jack Daniels for the pain," Jesse explained.

"But I don't drink," Marcy stated.

"Suit yourself, I would today though. I'll see you two in a little while. Larry and Ginger should be back soon."

"There they are now," Kat said, seeing Larry and Ginger walking out of the woods. The two walked up carrying two bottles of river water, and Jesse asked, "Did you find anything?"

"Only a river about a ten-minute walk from here and a new close friend," Ginger said, smiling at Larry.

"Really…" Kat said, looking at Jesse.

Jesse didn't say anything about that since he had too many things on his mind, setting Marcy's leg, getting Austin down, getting more water, and finding food since his belly was starting to growl. They explained to Larry and Ginger that Hugo had found a boy stuck in a tree, and they were about to go get him down.

"What can we do?" Ginger asked.

"Do you mind if you and Larry go back to the river and retrieve more water, as much as you can carry?" Jesse asked, "We really need some more water and maybe you can get the stainless steel champagne bucket I saw in the galley to boil it in. We should boil it a minute or two before we can drink it,"

Larry pointed to Ginger, "I told you he would know, and you need to boil it."

"You were right. We can do that, Jesse," Ginger replied.

"Sure, Doc, we can do that. I got nothing else going on," Larry repeated.

"Thanks. We're going to try to get this kid down," Jesse said, as he and Kat turned and followed Hugo into the woods. Ginger and Larry gathered containers to retrieve more water. Henry stacked up a couple of suitcases so Marcy could elevate her leg and then handed her the Tupperware with the Jack Daniels in it.

# Chapter 11

At the base of the giant sycamore tree where Austin was dangling, Jesse, Kat, and Hugo met up with Shu. Jesse and Hugo took the belts and buckled them together, forming one long belt. Jesse wrapped them around his waist about three times and then buckled the ends. He walked around the tree searching for the best climbing path to Austin. The tree's trunk was massive, and the first branch was a couple feet out of Jesse's reach, but just above it were plenty of climbing branches all the way to Austin. "Hugo, can you give me a boost?" Jesse asked.

Hugo leaned against the tree, locked his fingers, and held out his hands for Jesse to step into. Jesse placed one hand on Hugo's shoulder and the other on the tree and stepped into Hugo's hands. Hugo boosted him up, as he grabbed the lowest branch and heaved himself up onto it. Then Jesse began his cautious climb up to Austin.

"Did you guys find anything on your walk?" Shu asked Kat.

"Only some pecans," she answered.

"Still no sign of rescue planes?" Shu continued.

"None. Jesse has a theory, but I'll let him tell the whole group," Kat answered.

It took Jesse a good five minutes to reach Austin as he meticulously chose each foot and hand placement. He was standing on a limb that was about five feet out in front of Austin and a few feet higher. "Austin, hey my name's Jesse. Are you hurt?"

"No, just cold and really hungry," Austin answered.

"Hey Austin, what kind of tree fits in your hand?" Jesse asked.

"I don't know," Austin answered.

"A palm tree," Jesse stated, trying to loosen the mood a little and mask the fear for both of them.

Austin smiled and said, "That's lame, Jesse."

"I know, but it's the only tree joke I got. Well then, let's see if we can get you out of that seat. I want you to put this long belt around you and under your arms so you are holding it like this," Jesse explained, as he demonstrated how he wanted Austin to hold onto the belts. "I want you to wrap the long belt around you and buckle it to the rest, then wrap one hand around the belt strap and with the other release your seat belt when I say go. Push your armrest up and just let your body slide out. Can you do that?"

"Yes, I can do that," Austin answered.

"I'll be holding on to the other end, and I won't let you fall. I will swing you to the lower branch behind me. That one there, do you see it?" Jesse assured, as he pointed to the large branch below and behind him. "We won't do it until you're ready. Just let me know when you are."

Austin grabbed the belt end that Jesse swung over, and he wrapped it around him under his arms just as Jesse described. He unbuckled and re-buckled the belts cinching the long belt down to his chest. He twisted his fingers around the belt strap, reached down with his other hand, and touched the seat belt latch and looked at Jesse and said, "I'm ready, are you?"

Jesse tightened his grip on the belt strap and also twisted it around one arm. He checked his grip on the branch above him he was hanging onto, took up the slack in the belt strap, and said, "I got you, go."

"Here goes. Don't let me fall," Austin begged. With that, he released the seat belt latch and raised his arm rest. His body slid out, and Jesse felt the belts tighten to one another and the leather creaked as it squeezed his hand, causing it to hurt. He swung Austin to the designated branch, but Austin didn't get his footing and swung back away from the branch.

Jesse saw the belt he was holding was beginning to tear from being old and dry. He heaved Austin up and grabbed the belt below the tear with his other hand. "The belt is tearing!" he exclaimed. "Hold on! I have to move." Jesse twisted on his feet and faced the other direction and moved closer to the tree trunk. Leaning on the trunk, he squatted down and swung Austin to the limb. Austin got his footing and grabbed hold of a limb. Jesse let out a long sigh. "I'll climb down below you and spot you on the way down."

"I'm not afraid. You don't have to go out on a limb for me, let's branch out," Austin joked.

"Ha, ha, you're a funny man, aren't you? Be careful then, I'm right behind you," Jesse responded.

They both made it down the tree fairly quickly, and Austin dropped to the ground with Jesse right behind him. They stood and looked at each other, and Austin wrapped his arms around Jesse and gave him a hug then Hugo and Shu. He turned and looked at Kat and decided to give her a hug also. "Thank you for helping me. Do you have anything to eat, I'm starving?" he asked.

Kat handed him a handful of pecans she had shelled while watching him, and he scarfed them down. "I'm Kat, did you know the person in the seat next to you?" she asked.

"No, he was a stranger and never talked to me. I was catching some z's and listening to my earbuds when the plane started shaking. Then all of a sudden I saw sky and then I woke up next to the headless horseman. I had to steal his clothes to stay warm last night, but I'm still cold," he explained. "I need to call my mom. My phone was in the seat pouch in front of me; can I borrow yours?"

"None of them work, or we would let you," Shu responded.

"You mean none have service," Austin corrected.

"No, none work, they will not boot up or turn on," Shu added.

"Really... what's the deal?" Austin asked everyone.

"I don't know. I think it was a solar flare we flew through that made us crash and maybe took out our phones. Did you see the light show last night?" Jesse chimed in.

"I did, it was so cool but freaky. I didn't know what was going on," Austin answered. "How old are you, Austin?" Kat asked.

"Fourteen, how old are you?" he asked.

"I'm thirty-one," she answered.

"My mom's thirty-one; she had me when she was seventeen and still in high school. Okay, so I'll call her when we get to Atlanta then," he said.

"Uh Austin, we're in the Appalachian Mountains somewhere and help hasn't arrived yet. We were on the plane also. It might be a few days before we get there. Right now we're just waiting for help to arrive and trying to survive. We were looking for a house, a town, a way out of these woods and maybe food and a water source when we found you," Jesse admitted.

"Oh, she's going to go crazy. I'm all she has, dad left when I was a baby, and she's always worrying about me. She'll be coming to look for me," Austin declared.

"I hope so, Austin. I hope she sends help. Let's get you to the fire and find some warmer and cleaner clothes for you to wear," Kat assured. They all studied the oversized, blood stained jacket and extra shirt Austin was wearing. They walked back to camp together, explaining to him who survived and what had been going on to get him up to speed.

# Chapter 12

Marcy screamed as Jesse pushed suddenly on her leg and with a loud crack her bone ends were forced to meet into place, so they would heal properly. She had drunk some Jack Daniels and had a good buzz going but the pain was too much, and she passed out. Jesse re-splinted her leg and elevated it to alleviate further swelling. Austin looked on in amazement, as Jesse checked Marcy's vitals. Everyone was kicking around solar flare scenarios for the cause of the crash, the cause of that light show, and why help had not arrived yet. They wondered how long they should stand around and wait, and what if help never comes. They could starve to death. These were some of the things discussed and argued over at length with no resolve.

Tension was rising as apprehensions set in while the day drug on and still no sign of rescue. Hungry bellies growled, and the cold was constant with no place to escape the wind or the chill. They tried to keep busy by gathering more fire wood and looking for more things to use for their survival but the constant presence of dead bodies lying around was a morale breaker. Henry wanted to gather all the bodies and move them into the tail of the plane but the argument was they were evidence and shouldn't be moved. Larry, Jesse, Kat, and Hugo agreed that the energy it would take to move all the bodies would take its toll on them without having food to eat to replenish their strength. They felt like they were stuck in limbo and could only wait for help that may never come. The waiting was driving them crazy. Living in a society with such great distractions as smart phones, notebooks, laptops, and wifi, they didn't know what to do with themselves without them.

"I think we should leave now," Larry bellowed.

"What about Marcy, she can't walk, and it could be miles out of here," Jesse objected.

"We could make one of those lean-to things and drag her out of here, you know, like in western movies," Hugo added.

"Yeah Doc, one of those," Larry approved.

"You mean a travois. Are one of you going to drag it with her on it, up and down hollows, over mountains, across creeks and rivers, through bushes and thickets?" Jesse ranted.

"We get your point, Doc," Larry concluded. "Well, Ginger and I can go, and we'll send help back."

"Don't get me into this. I'm staying with Jesse," Ginger chimed in. Larry got a disappointed look on his face, and she said, pointing at the woods, "You know you wouldn't last out there."

Larry thought for a moment, as everyone was anticipating a derogatory comeback, but instead, he said, "Yeah, you're right."

"So what do you suggest?" Hugo asked.

"We wait, at least until tomorrow to see if help does come. At least by then Marcy might be able to walk with a crutch, and we can all walk out of here together," Jesse advised.

"Are we just supposed to starve for two days?" Austin cut in, concerned. "I'm a growing boy, I need my carbs."

"No, we can fish, hunt, and trap. We can go fish the river and make some snares for rabbits or squirrels. I also have the marshal's pistol, and if we have to, we can shoot a small animal for food," Jesse proposed. "It's not ideal, but it will feed us. I have three collapsible rods, two fly reels and a Zebco 33, in my suitcase. Let's go catch some fish. Kat and Austin would you like to join me?"

"Heck yeah!" Austin exclaimed.

"Anyone can come of course. We still need more water. And if we can't catch any, someone else should try," Jesse added.

"We'll go with you, we've been to the river twice already," Ginger volunteered herself and Larry.

At the river, Jesse gave the Zebco 33 rod and reel to Austin with a yellow rooster tail lure tied on and let him fish the slower pool areas of the river. "Reel it fast enough to keep it off the bottom but slow enough not to outrun the fish. Also, run it up the edges of the rocks and the bank in the deepest parts. The fish will be hiding there," Jesse instructed. He gave a fly rod and reel to Ginger and Larry and demonstrated to them and Kat how to fly cast using the back and forth motion for fly fishing. "Trout stay in the whitewater for the most oxygen, so this is where you want to fish. Stay clear of the overhanging branches. Take your time and focus on where you want the fly to land. Most times when it hits the water or not long after that is when you'll get the strike. The fish are watching for food and will react quickly. When you get a strike, tighten the line with a jerk and always keep tension on it all the way until you have the fish in your hand. This will insure he doesn't get off, and remember you are fishing for your supper. I'll try to assist whoever hooks one."

They fished for about an hour, and Kat caught two brook trout about fourteen inches long, enough to feed her and Jesse for one meal. Ginger caught a nice, smallmouth bass after getting hung up several times. Larry tried but never got a bite. The bass was about two pounds and would be plenty for them and maybe one or two of the others. Austin hadn't had any luck and decided to walk out on a section of rocks sticking up in hopes of catching one. He cast the rooster tail in front of a large rock submerged just under the water and let it sink a second and bam, a strike. Austin jerked back on his rod to set the hook. He was so excited that he had finally hooked a fish. He felt something hit him and fell backward into the frigid water. He turned the rod loose and the shock of the cold took him by surprise. He took in a big gulp of icy water and began to choke and fight for his life as the current sent him down river.

Kat looked up and around to find Austin. She didn't see him and then noticed something floating by her and realized it was Austin. She screamed, "Jesse! Austin has fallen into the river!"

Larry and Ginger looked up and saw him struggling to swim. Larry was closest to him and began to run along the river bank to try to catch up and help him. The current became swift, and it plunged Austin to the bottom. He smacked his face on a rock, and it nearly knocked him unconscious. He shoved off with his hands and then flipped over on his back. His head popped out, and he gasped for a breath of air only for it to be ripped away with another violent plunge to the bottom. He became disoriented and didn't know which way was up or down. His arms and legs began to throb from the cold, and they felt very heavy and hard to move. Water had begun to fill his lungs and breathing was becoming difficult.

Larry ran as fast as he could to get in front of Austin. When he did, he ran and dove into the river hoping to get into position to retrieve Austin, but he only found himself in distress for help also. The water was so cold, and the current was so strong; it just pushed him downstream. He thought what have I done?

Jesse ran behind Larry, and when he saw him enter the river and how quickly he struggled, he yelled," Get on your back, feet downstream! Get on your back, feet downstream!"

Larry heard Jesse and flipped over on his back and put his feet downstream and was able to stop himself on a large rock. He turned and looked for Austin, as the boy floated by just out of reach. Larry pushed off with his feet to grab Austin; he was so close but just couldn't make contact.

Austin was barely moving and his head was under water. As his life ebbed away from him, he thought of his mom. Will she ever know what happened to me? Will she find my body? Will I see dad in heaven? He gave into the cold and surrendered the fight for the struggle was too hard and his heart ceased to beat. His limp body floated down river like a log.

Larry made one more last ditch effort to catch Austin, and he swam as hard he could to reach him. He finally felt him and grabbed his pant leg and drew him up. Larry flipped Austin over to get his face out the water, as he turned on his back with his feet facing downstream. He saw a sandbar coming up and tried to make his way to it. He saw Jesse step down onto the sandbar with a long branch and heard him yelling to grab the branch. Larry grabbed hold of the limb with one hand and held tightly to Austin with the other. Jesse pulled them both up and out of the water.

Ginger was yelling Larry's name as she and Kat were right behind Jesse and helped him pull them both out of the water. Jesse began CPR on Austin, and in-between breaths told Kat to quickly make a fire. "I don't have a lighter," she declared.

"Who has it?" Jesse asked.

"Larry," she answered.

"Check his pockets for the lighter; I left mine with Henry," Jesse said.

"I can't find it," Kat said, as she felt each of Larry's pockets.

Larry was blue from being in the water and was shaking and then he passed out. "He's going into hypothermic shock. He needs to be warmed up quickly or he'll die. Take his clothes off!" Jesse shouted. After about five minutes of CPR, Jesse knew Austin wasn't coming back and made the decision to save Larry's life. Jesse dug out a big area with his hands digging away leaves and sticks and even scratched into the dirt some. He stood up and stripped down to his underwear and said, "Take off your clothes, now."

Ginger's eyes got real big, and she looked at Kat.

"Larry needs our body heat to survive. Skin on skin is the best form of body heat. You can leave your underwear on but take off the rest and then put your jackets back on. But be sure to open them up when you lay on Larry." Jesse sprinkled his spot with leaves and drug Larry over to it. He laid down in it on his back and pulled Larry on top of him. "Ginger, you're next. Lay on top of him to one side. Kat, place our clothes over her and to that side, bunch up the leaves too. Then you lie on the other side and put the rest of the clothes over you."

Ginger stripped down to her pink lacy bra and removed her pants. "Sorry, I go commando, you know, panty lines," she said, as she lay down on Larry as Jesse instructed. Kat furrowed her eyebrows and placed some clothes over Ginger's legs and scooted leaves up to their sides. Kat stripped down to her sports bra and Hello Kitty panties and also lay down on Larry as Jesse instructed, covering herself up to the best of her ability. They all four laid there in a tight bundle as each of them hugged each other to warm Larry's core temperature.

"How long do have to be this way?" Kat asked.

"Until he wakes up," Jesse answered. "I'm sorry but this was only way."

"I'm sorry about Austin," Kat said.

"Yeah, me too," Jesse agreed.

After several minutes passed in silence, Ginger begged, "Come on Larry, wake up. You have two naked women on you, every man's dream. Please, wake up."

Yeah, come on Larry, wake up. You are naked on top of a naked man," Jesse whispered and grunted from the weight of the three on top of him. "I thought that might wake him even quicker than the other."

They all three laughed but their laughter quickly faded in realization of their dire situation. They just saved Austin and then lost him again. Larry may not make it, and they were still in need of food, shelter, and rescue. "What happened to the fish?" Jesse asked.

"I dropped them somewhere, nearby where we were fishing. I'm sure I could find them again," Kat answered.

After about fifteen minutes, Larry groaned. They couldn't make out what he said. His words were slurred. "I think he's waking up," Jesse said.

Larry raised his head and saw Jesse's face under him and noticed that they didn't have on any shirts and he said, "What the... Doc!"

"Calm down, we saved your life," Jesse coughed.

Larry realized that Ginger and Kat were laying on him, and they were all nearly naked as warmth and feeling began to return to his body. "Well, how about that Doc." Larry gave Jesse a big kiss on his cheek. "I just want to thank you for this wonderful foursome."

"Get up! Get him off me!" Jesse shouted.

Kat and Ginger stood up, and Larry rolled off of Jesse still not being able to stand. He looked at Kat and Ginger and declared, "Woo, hoo! What a treat!"

"Can it perv, we saved your life," Kat scolded.

"What about Austin; did he make it?" Larry looked around and saw Austin lying in the leaves lifeless. "Ah, crap!" Larry exclaimed.

They all looked at each other feeling the loss, and Jesse said, "We still need to rub his extremities to get the blood flowing good again. He's not out of the woods yet, no pun intended. It's still very cold out here, and all his clothes are wet."

Ginger, Kat, and Jesse put their clothes back on, and Jesse gave his coat and under shirt to Larry so he could gird himself. They rubbed his arms, hands, legs, and feet to get the blood circulating well and the warmth returned to them. They hurried back to find the fish and retrieve the rods and reels. The Zebco was lost, and they couldn't find the fish. "We gotta go. We've got to get Larry to the fire; it will be dark soon," Jesse admitted.

They all walked back to camp, carrying as much water as they could and stopping along the way to warm up Larry's feet, legs, and hands. "Please don't tell the others you saw me naked," Kat fretted.

"We didn't, just your Hello Kitty panties," Jesse laughed.

"I wasn't expecting for anyone to see those. They're comfortable, and when you're on a plane you want to be comfortable," she added.

"No judgement, I had a naked Larry on top of me," Jesse admitted.

"You loved it, Doc," Larry poked.

"Let's all agree to not to speak of those naked moments," Ginger convinced.

"Agreed!" They all said in unison.

# Chapter 13

Everyone sat quietly around the fire as the news of Austin sunk in. Ginger found Larry some clothes from a suitcase, jeans, and a t-shirt with a unicorn on it that read, *I poop rainbows.* Larry was of small stature so they were probably women's clothes, but they fit like a glove. She also found him some tennis shoes and a coat. They all pilfered through the suitcases and layered up on clothes since it was cold, and they were talking about walking out of the woods.

"Should we keep the same watch as last night?" Hugo asked the group.

"That's fine with me, everyone okay with that?" Jesse answered.

Everyone nodded their heads except Larry. He seemed as though he was in a world of his own and not listening to anyone, he sat staring into the fire.

"Larry! Larry!" Jesse raised his voice to get his attention, but Larry never looked up.

Ginger nudged Larry with her elbow, and he looked up at her, and she motioned to Jesse.

"What?" He asked, turning to Jesse.

"Tonight's watch, same as last night? I want you to get a good night's sleep since your body had a traumatic event happen to it," Jesse said.

"Yeah, yeah," he responded and went back to staring into the fire.

Jesse got up and went over to Larry and sat next to him. "Larry, it's not your fault. Austin was dead before you ever entered the water. Don't blame yourself. It's just…"

"What? Fate? Austin was just a boy. Why would he survive this plane crash only to drown in a river just a day later?" Larry cut in.

"I don't know, Larry, but you were heroic today. The elements were just stacked against us. We're all very proud of what you tried to do for Austin, but you can't blame yourself," Jesse urged.

"Thanks Doc, you know, for what you did for me today," Larry offered.

"You're welcome. I don't take my clothes off for just anybody," he whispered, jokingly patting Larry on the back.

Larry smiled a half smile and said, "You know, that's been the story of my whole life, always a little too late."

Jesse didn't respond and not knowing what to say to that he kept quiet and waited for Larry to add to his comment, but he never said anything else.

Nighttime came and everyone's bellies growled, and all the food they had found was gone. Marcy had finished off the Jack Daniels, and Jesse gave her the rest of the aspirin from the first aid kit for her pain, and she fell sound asleep. Henry bedded down knowing his watch was coming and wanted to get some sleep. Hugo and Shu weren't talking much so they laid down to sleep in hopes tomorrow would be better than the last. Ginger and Larry were cuddled under a large beach towel with their heads laid over on each other. Kat and Jesse for the second night began their watch together.

"Is Larry having a hard time with Austin's death?" Kat asked.

"Yeah, I think we all are. It is hard to swallow. He was just here, and he's gone and after surviving being thrown from the plane like that. I get why Larry's blaming himself, but it was not his fault. If anyone is to blame, it's me. I shouldn't have let him gone fishing," he answered.

"No, it wasn't your fault either. You could not have known he was going to fall into the water," she affirmed.

"I should have kept my eye on him, he was only fourteen."

"Yes fourteen, he was very capable of taking care of himself. He was on the flight by himself. It was a freak thing that happened. It's not anyone's fault," she declared.

"I know you're right, but we're surrounded by so much death; it's starting to wear on me," he admitted. "I'm just ready to go home."

"That makes eight of us." After several silent minutes, she asked, "Where is home?"

"Acworth, Georgia."

"I know where that is. I have a friend that lives in Woodstock."

"I have seven acres near Lake Allatoona."

"So, we're not that far from one another."

"No, Atlanta is about twenty-five minutes on a weekend, but about an hour during the week with all the traffic and road work."

"Yes I know, it has gotten bad with all that construction," she agreed.

"Do you miss the country, living in the city?"

"I do. I want to move to the burbs, but a magazine I write for is right down the street. I would move if there were a good reason to, you know for someone," she admitted.

Jesse nodded his head and noticed something moving in the fire light at the edge of camp. He shined his flashlight toward the movement and saw a coyote lurking around. "Another coyote, we can't keep them away. There are too many free meals around here. If we get real hungry, we can have coyote stew. I hear it tastes like chicken."

"It does, like dark meat."

"What? You've had coyote?"

"Yeah, dad cooked it one year when our crops were damaged by a storm, and we were broke. He killed it in our chicken house. It had killed some of our best layers, so he said we were going to eat it."

"Was it good?"

"I was young, but I remember it being tough and tasting a lot like a drumstick. Does that change the way you look at me?"

"How do I look at you?"

"I don't know, like a lady," she held up quotations with her finger when she said the word lady.

"Not at all, that happened when I saw you in those Hello Kitty panties."

"Stop it! We all agreed."

"I know, but I couldn't resist. I just can't get those out my mind, the coyotes, I mean," he said, clearing his throat.

They both looked at each other and chuckled a little, "Come on let's see where it's going," Jesse suggested.

They both followed the animal at a distance to see where it was headed. It went to the same body that Henry shooed it away from the night before. Jesse threw several rocks at it with much effort, and it finally ran off into the woods. They walked over to the body, and when Kat saw that the face and arm had been peeled away by the coyote's canines, she gasped and put her hand over her mouth. "This should not be happening. Why haven't they found us?" she questioned.

"I don't know, but if help doesn't come tomorrow, we're walking out of here," he announced.

# Chapter 14

Jesse woke Hugo and Shu for their watch, and he and Kat bedded down by the fire. Hugo yawned and rubbed his face with both of his hands. He took the flashlights Jesse gave him and handed one to Shu. They both walked the area perimeter to check for predators and then stopped by the tail of the plane. Something caught Hugo's eye; he reached down and picked it up. It was a strip of three photos of Dan and Marcy making funny faces taken in a photo booth. He stared at the photos for a moment and then handed them to Shu. "They look so happy. I get it, Shu. I'll leave Maria, and we can get married."

"No!" she said in a forceful whisper. "You're not leaving Maria; this is something I have to do. I feel dirty, and I lost my best friend. I can't look her in the face. When my parents died, she was there for me; when she had your kids, I was there for her. It's just not about you and me; it's about doing what's right. I can't be a part of your family anymore; it's wrong. I love you, Hugo, but it's just wrong."

"Why? Why is it wrong if we all love each other?"

"Because Hugo, you're not all mine, and you're not all Maria's. I don't think that's how it's supposed to be, sneaking around, hiding, lying to people we love. You don't lie to the people you love."

"It never bothered you before; even in business deals, you're like a shark."

"I know, but it's bothering me now. My life has flashed before my eyes, and I'm so disappointed in what I see. I don't want to be that person anymore. If I would've died on that plane, I would have been forgotten. My life has had no substance to it, business deals, numbers and one long affair, nothing of value."

"You're valuable to me."

"But not valuable enough for you to have married me twenty years ago or any year since."

"Shu, you know I love you. I told you I would leave Maria and marry you. I still need you for my...*our* business."

"No, it's too late. We have to be together to get back home, but then, I'm done."

"I'm going to give you some space, and we can discuss it again in Texas. You might feel different in our own environment. Out here, it's scary and unknown, and we've seen a lot of people die. Even Austin's death has shaken me some, and I told you I would leave Maria for you, Shu. Just think about it, please. Don't decide out here." They finished out their watch in silence only speaking when necessary. They woke Henry and Ginger and fell asleep by the fire.

# Chapter 15

Henry stoked the fire for the group, then he and Ginger stepped away. "Are you ready for this again?" Henry asked.

"Ready as I'll ever be," she answered.

"Let's go for a walk," he declared.

"I'm so hungry," she said.

"Me too, my belly has been growling all night. I should've had that sandwich on the plane."

"So, you've been a preacher for half a century?"

"Yep, that's right."

"Do you have any white people in your church since you're…?"

"You can say it, black or African American if you prefer. I'm a black man. And yes, we do have some white folks and even some interracial families that attend. In fact, one of my deacons is a white man married to a black woman. Why do you ask?"

"I don't know, it's just white and black people tend not to gather together, especially in churches."

"Well, you're right about that, but I think it's the cultures and not the color."

"Oh, okay. Do you have any redheads in your church?"

Henry snickered and said, "No, I don't think we do. Does that make us prejudice against redheads?"

"No, it just means you're missing out."

He snickered some more, "You're probably right."

"Was that you're belly growling?"

"It was. Maybe we can rustle up some breakfast at daybreak."

"Maybe, God-willing and the creek don't rise."

"Amen sister! Amen."

Henry and Ginger had an uneventful watch as they carried on conversations about all kinds of things. Ginger would just throw out a thought, and they would discuss their views and whisper debate and even comical thoughts about each topic. She kept Henry on his toes and his mind off his hunger. Ginger was a very curious person, and they became good friends overnight. Henry admired her curiosity and thought it would guide her well in life. Ginger looked up to Henry and admired him for dedicating his life to God and to serving people. She saw him as a grandfather and a very wise old man. She lay back down by the fire with Larry, and Henry woke Jesse for the night's final watch.

"Goodnight, Henry," Ginger whispered.

"Goodnight, Ginger."

# Chapter 16

Jesse rose slowly from the lack of sleep, food, and stress of the days prior. The cold didn't help with matters either. It had been two days since the crash, and they still hadn't found any provisions of substance. Even though he knew they could survive without food for a few weeks, they needed it for energy for the walk out. He didn't know how far or how long it would take, but he knew he needed to get some grub for everyone. Henry and Jesse checked the area and then ended up at the body that the coyote had been eating. "Have you seen that coyote lately?" Jesse asked.

"No, Ginger and I didn't see any animals."

"We need to find some food. We're going to need the energy. I might go fishing again at first light. If we make a trap, we might be able to catch a squirrel or two."

"Whatever you think," Henry said. He had seen that Jesse was trustworthy and had everyone's best interests at heart.

"I thought about shooting that coyote if I saw it again. What do you think?"

"I ate dog in Nam. If that's all God provides, I'm game."

"Okay, coyote might be on the menu."

"Just make sure we cook it completely, well done. We don't want to get sick."

"Copy that," Jesse agreed.

They made several sweeps of the camp in hopes of the coyote showing itself but it never did. The sun began to rise, and Jesse said, "I'm going to slip off and try to catch some fish. I'll be back in about two hours or so, hopefully with breakfast."

"Okay, I'll send up a prayer and let the others know."

Jesse was gone for about two and a half hours and came back with three large brook trout, weighing about three pounds each. Everyone was so excited that they were finally going to get something to eat. Hugo made some Y-shaped sticks to hold the fish. Jesse gutted the fish and ran a stick through their gills and stabbed it through their tails to hold them in place. He set the Y-shaped sticks over the open flames to cook. "Okay, in about fifteen minutes, we'll have some good protein to eat."

Everyone cheered and waited, looking on with watering mouths and hunger pains in their stomachs. Once the trout was done, they all gobbled down pieces of fish, picking at the bones. "I think we should leave this afternoon. With those dark, gray clouds rolling in, snow might be in the forecast, if help hasn't come by then," Jesse announced.

"What about Marcy? How is she going to walk on that leg?" Shu asked.

"I'm going to make her some crutches. Maybe it won't be that far out of here," Jesse added. "Marcy, how do you feel? Can you walk on some crutches?"

"I think so. My leg hurts, but as long as I don't put my weight on it, I think I can," Marcy answered.

"Well, we'll have to help you up hills and through difficult areas," Kat assured.

"Thank you guys for taking care of me. But before we go, can Henry do a short memorial for Dan and the others left here?" Marcy asked. "I don't know how long it will be until..." she teared up.

"Sure, I can," Henry agreed.

"So we're all in agreement to leave this afternoon?" Jesse asked the group.

"What if we miss our rescue?" Shu asked, "What if help comes after we leave?"

"Help hasn't come, and we don't know if it will. We can leave a note letting them know we left," Hugo suggested.

"That's a great idea; we'll do that. Will that make everyone feel better?" Jesse asked.

Everyone was in agreement. They gathered items that they thought were important. They made piles of stuff according to what it was so that they could make final decisions on what to take when they packed each bag for carrying. They piled up women's clothes, men's clothes, shoes, toiletries, and several backpacks from the luggage and carry-on bags.

Larry snatched up a wrapped Christmas present and tore into it and said, "I think we should check these out before we leave. Look, it's an electric razor, Merry Christmas, Doc." He tossed it to Jesse. He picked up another gift and gave it to Ginger and then handed all of them out. They all tore into them as though it was Christmas morning and Santa had just left them under their tree. They didn't find many useful items for their survival. It was mostly generic gifts and souvenir-type stuff with a few toys mixed in. They all had a disappointed look on their faces, after opening so many presents and not finding anything to use.

They all packed a bag from their own stuff and from the piles they had made. "Remember to keep it light. We don't know how far we have to travel. Just think about warmth and survival, anything else is just dead weight," Jesse announced. "Marcy, you will have to share a bag or spread stuff out over several of our bags since you can't carry one."

"Shu and I are sharing," Marcy responded.

After everyone was packed up, Jesse and Hugo had fashioned some crutches out of limbs with Jesse's knives and they gave them to Marcy to test out. "Try these," Hugo said, handing the crutches to her.

Marcy checked the crutches for fit, but they had to be adjusted in length by shortening them a little. After the third adjustment and wrapping the tops with folded up clothes, they seemed to work well for Marcy. She shuffled around camp a bit to get used to them. She knew it was going to be a hard, slow journey but was also glad to be leaving the horror behind.

They all gathered by the tail of the plane for final words over the dead. Hugo and Jesse placed Dan's body in the fuselage as far as they could. Upon exiting, Henry said, "'And I heard a voice from heaven saying unto me, blessed are the dead which die in the Lord, that they may rest from their labors. I know that my Redeemer liveth and mine eyes shall behold Him.' We brought nothing into this world and it is certain, we can take nothing out. So we commit these dead to the ground, ashes to ashes, and dust to dust."

After a short prayer, Henry concluded the service, and when Marcy had composed herself, they all began their journey through the woods in hopes of making it back home.

# Chapter 17

They had decided to walk east, thinking they might run into a town and if not a town, a house, and if they kept going east, they would eventually run into the coast. Their chances were better going east than any other direction since they knew they would eventually leave Appalachia. The sun had been hidden behind dark and gray clouds all afternoon. The threat of snow was looming, and they were eager to find shelter for the night. After a couple of hours of slow walking with Marcy struggling to keep up, Jesse said, "Let's take a break."

They all dropped their bags and plopped down to get a drink. Marcy leaned against a tree and slid down as Shu helped her to sit. Shu handed their bag to Marcy, and she dug through it, looking for some more aspirin, but instead, she found the photo of her and Dan. "I put that in there for you," Shu said.

Marcy teared up and said, "Thank you."

"Hugo found it on the ground, and I thought you might want to keep it," Shu added.

Marcy tucked the photo into her pocket and wiped the tears off her face and said, "Jesse, my leg hurts really bad, do we have any more aspirin?"

"Sorry, we don't. But let me take a look at it, maybe the splint is too tight," Jesse answered. He un-wrapped the splint, exposing her lower leg, and it was a light blueish purple color. "It looks like your leg is on the mend. There's a little less swelling, but it will hurt for days and maybe a week or two. Broken bones are painful, I know. I broke my arm once, and it hurt for about two weeks, even after some, when I bumped my cast. Let's rest for about fifteen minutes, and then I'll re-splint it for you."

"Do we have anything else for pain? It's aching so much. It's starting to make me sick to my stomach," Marcy whined.

"I'll look," he responded. He dug through the first aid bag that he had combined from the two kits, leaving some of the bulky items behind. "All I have is some Lidocaine which is topical and wouldn't help much. I'm sorry, but you will have to push through the pain. Elevate it while you rest."

"I have some Jim Beam, two little bottles I found in the galley before we left," Larry offered, pulling one from his bag.

"I don't think that's a good idea with you on crutches," Jesse advised Marcy.

"I have to have something. My leg is killing me. I'll only drink half the bottle. Maybe it will take the edge off the pain," she suggested.

"Alright, you're an adult, but I don't recommend it. It could diminish your balance," Jesse argued.

Marcy took the Jim Beam bottle and turned it up, consuming a little more than half and then breathed out heavy as the burn of the whiskey took her breath away. Everyone laughed at her, as she had quickly forgotten the Jack Daniels' burn from the day before.

"My dad called it fire water, and he said it has demons in it. That's why they call it spirits, he claimed," Hugo said. "He'd say, 'If you drink too much, you'll drink away the angels', but it didn't stop me from drinking. I think it was just his way of trying to deter me."

Marcy caught her breath, wiped her mouth, and handed the bottle back to Larry, "Thanks."

"No problem," Larry smiled. He turned to Hugo and asked, "Do you want a drink?" Hugo held up his hand to decline. Larry placed the bottle back in his bag.

"We leave in ten," Jesse announced.

Kat approached Jesse and asked, "Is she going to make it?"

"I hope so. Her leg is okay for now. If she's careful on it, she'll make it," Jesse explained. "We need to find a place to camp for the night. Those clouds look threatening, and we don't have much of daylight left. I don't think Marcy will do to well in the dark."

"I don't think any of us will do well in the dark out here. There's too much to trip on," Kat agreed.

"Hey Jesse, look," Hugo pointed to something far off in the distance.

Jesse stepped up next to Hugo, and everyone else joined them except Marcy. They peered out over the treetops and saw what might be a house, a barn, or shack.

"We're saved!" Ginger announced. "There's a house over there!" She started jumping up and down with Larry.

"Hold on, Ginger. We don't know what that is so don't get your hopes up too high. But yeah, we're close to civilization!" Jesse smiled, as he also got excited that they might soon be getting out of this grisly ordeal.

Everyone began to celebrate the discovery and was excited and anxious to get there. "How far do you think that is, Henry?" Jesse asked.

"At least a mile, maybe two, it's a long way from here," Henry calculated.

"It's definitely way over a mile," Jesse admitted. "It will take us at least an hour to get there with Marcy and just before nightfall. Plus, we need to get down that with her." Jesse pointed at the steep rock-filled ridge they would have to go down.

They all gathered their bags and began to slowly maneuver their way down the ridge. "Slow and easy, slow and easy," Jesse cautioned Marcy, as he and Hugo tried to spot her on their way down together. Jesse planted his foot against a rock, but the rock gave way, making him slip and fall on to his bottom. He slid down the ridge several yards before he could stop himself.

Marcy took her focus off what she was doing and leaned forward too far and fell head first down the ridge. She screamed and upon the first impact against the frozen rocky ground, her body fell limp and slid to a stop near the bottom.

Hugo had reached out to try and grab her, but he missed for she was just out of his reach as he steadied himself to keep from falling as well. "Marcy!" he yelled.

Everyone stopped and watched as if in slow motion as her body rode on dirt and debris until she was halted by gathered rocks close to the bottom of the ridge. "Oh my God!" Kat screamed.

Jesse made it to Marcy first, but she wasn't moving. He looked at her and knew from the color of her skin that her blood had quit pumping. Her nose was red earlier when they spoke and now it was white and her eyes were empty. He felt her neck, and it was broken. He knew she was dead. He laid his head on her stomach and began to weep. He looked up and shouted to the sky as if shouting at God. "Will this nightmare ever end?"

Kat made it over to them, and she squatted down and placed her hand on Jesse's back. "Oh, Marcy," she whispered. "This is not your fault, Jesse."

"Yeah? Then why do people keep dying on my watch?" he ranted.

"This is not your watch! This is us, all of us, trying to get home. We all just ended up together," Kat barked. "Austin and Marcy are no one's fault. It just is."

"That's right, son, this is not your fault. She had a broken leg, and God chose to take her home to be with Dan," Henry agreed.

Jesse composed himself and said, "Let's cover her up at least."

Shu pulled out a blanket from their bag and went to Marcy to cover her and noticed the photo sticking out of her pocket. She bent down and pulled it out. She looked at it and thought of how happy they appeared, and then she thought of how happy she was just a couple of days ago. She laid the photo on Marcy's chest and placed a small rock on it so it wouldn't blow away and then covered her with the blanket.

# Chapter 18

They could see the structure as the light began to slowly fade. Tiny snowflakes had just begun to fall, and they had walked in near silence since leaving Marcy lying under a blanket. No one knew what to say, especially to Jesse. He took Marcy's death hard, feeling somewhat responsible since he was spotting her; plus, it was his idea to leave. Maybe she needed another day to heal, or maybe help came, but they were already gone from the crash site, he thought. Maybe he jumped the gun in leaving. Maybe he should have made a travois after all. These were things Jesse turned over and over in his mind as they walked. "Second-guessing gets you nowhere," he whispered to himself, a phrase pounded into his head as a combat medic by his lieutenant.

"People will die. You save the ones you can, forget the ones you can't; let your boys bring'em home," Lieutenant Chandler would say. "You got that, Sergeant Gibson? Is that clear?"

"Crystal, sir," Jesse whispered to himself, as he gave himself a pep talk to get his mind back on track. Even though his lieutenant told him to forget the ones he couldn't save, Jesse remembered each one that had died in front of him, even those he had to kill to protect his unit. His mind's eye flashed back to an IED explosion that went off, killing two of his men while they fell under attack by several insurgents. He had to defend himself and the lives of those in his unit by taking the lives of those that attacked them. The rebels were just kids, not even sixteen years old and already brainwashed into killing machines. He and his men were pinned down with heavy fire, and he was the only one in a position to take them out. He remembered their young faces, and he hated what he had to do. He saw something lying on the ground several yards in front of the cabin that pulled his mind away from that regretful moment. He stopped and signaled everyone to halt.

"What is it?" Kat asked.

"It looks like a body," Jesse guessed, as he was pretty sure he saw a man's face.

"What? A body?" Hugo pushed by Kat and peered at the lump on the ground.

"Heads up people, something is shady here," Jesse warned.

Hugo and Jesse walked slowly to the lump alone and found that it was indeed the body of a man wearing a ghillie suit, and he had been shot in the chest. "What's going on?" Hugo asked.

"I don't know but take cover while I clear the cabin," Jesse warned. He motioned for everyone to hide as Hugo filled them in.

Jesse drew the Sig Sauer P229 from its holster, checked the chamber for a round and clicked the safety off. He approached the front door with caution, reached for the door knob and turned it. It was unlocked, and he swung the door open. He quickly glanced into the cabin for hostiles, and then he stormed in with his gun trained forward. He found a dead body sitting in a chair in a corner with sunglasses on and holding an empty beer can, but no one else. "It's okay guys!" he shouted toward the door.

They all stepped in and stared at the body. "I think this is Jack or Jon," Jesse admitted.

"That's Jon," Kat declared. "Remember the guy who helped us get Larry out."

"Oh yeah, you're right, it is," Hugo piped in. "What the heck?"

"I think this cabin belongs to that dead guy out there and Jon or maybe Jack killed him. Question is, where is Jack now?" Jesse pondered. "Looks like the snowflakes are getting bigger; I guess this is home for the night. Let's move Jon out with the other guy and get a fire going in that stove there."

They moved Jon's stiff body outside and laid him down next to the ghillie suit man. Jesse and Hugo retrieved wood from out front, and Henry built a fire in the wood burning stove that was on the east side and in the center of the wall. The cabin was about a twenty foot by fourteen foot room with an old brown couch that folded out into a bed and one oddly outdated lounge chair that sat in the corner. There was a sink with no running water; a small pan rack overhead with several pots and pans hanging from it. Shelves lined the west wall which was very sparingly stocked with canned food, ammo, water, and toiletries. There was a fold-down table on the north wall with two straight-back chairs and a small window giving up what little light was left. Several clear, mason jars sat around the room with used candles in them. A black bearskin rug hung on the south wall by the door along with a few sets of whitetail deer antlers.

After they warmed themselves by the stove and the heat chased away the chill in the cabin, Jesse said, "Let's check out the perimeter and see what we can find, and if there's any signs of Jack."

"Shu and I are going to try to whip us up a candlelight dinner out of this," Kat announced, as she picked up a can of corn and a can of hominy.

"That sounds wonderful," Jesse replied with his eyebrows raised.

"Yea, I'm starving. I'll help too," Ginger added.

"Okay guys, let's let the ladies do their thing," Henry said.

The four men stepped out of the cabin and closed the door behind them. Hugo turned on his flashlight and shown it all around. The snow had dusted the ground, but now it was barely falling. He pointed his light toward what looked like a carport or shed. They stepped up under it, and Hugo spotted a dirt bike, "Hey, there's a motorcycle," he announced.

"Maybe we can crank it and someone can ride for help," Larry suggested.

"Not without the chain," Hugo said, pointing to an empty rusted sprocket.

"Maybe it's lying around here somewhere," Henry hoped.

They looked all around but found no chain, just a box of wrenches and sockets along with some old miscellaneous motorcycle parts. "Let's check the back," Jesse said. They searched the back, but there was no chain and no sign of Jack anywhere.

"You think Jack's still around here?" Larry asked.

"If he's smart, he would be long gone by now. I'm sure the Feds are wondering why their prisoners haven't made it to Atlanta yet and have sent out a search posse. But I'm not sure about his brother; Jack might be back for his body," Jesse answered with concern.

"We can lock and barricade the door, and the window is too small for anyone to come through, so we should all be able to get some sleep tonight," Hugo added.

"It would be nice to be able to sleep through the night," Jesse said. "You know we could just let Larry pull an all-nighter."

"Sounds good to me," Hugo agreed.

"I'll second that," Henry piped in.

"Hey! Doc, you didn't want me to pull watch," Larry defended.

"I know, we're just jabbing you," Jesse joked. "Let's go see what the ladies whipped up."

# Chapter 19

Kat found a can opener and opened a can of hominy and a can of corn then poured them both into a pan. "See if there is any sugar around here and some salt and pepper," Kat asked.

"I found some sugar," Ginger announced, turning and handing the container of sugar to Kat.

"Try this, you can make creamed corn," Shu said, holding up a can of cream of chicken soup.

"Nice! Here's the opener," Kat said, handing it to Shu. Kat poured in some sugar and eyeballed the amount, stirring it in as Shu poured in the soup.

"Here's some salt and pepper," Ginger said after finding shakers sitting on the window seal.

"Sprinkle some in, and we'll let it heat up a while," Kat directed.

"So, you like Jesse?" Ginger asked.

"What? He's nice and all; he's helping us get home," Kat answered.

"I see the way you look at him. He looks at you too, you know," Ginger admitted.

"Yeah, I've noticed that too. The way you two do things together, and he always wants you to be with him when he goes off or does something," Shu added.

"Stop, you guys. Okay, I like him. There's something about him that… He's so manly," Kat expressed.

"Yeah, he's hot,"

"Ginger! He is, right," Kat beamed.

"He does have that sexy middle-aged masculine look going for him; he seems to be very intelligent," Shu agreed.

"We see the sparks flying between you two," Ginger affirmed.

"This is almost ready. Try it. Careful, it's hot," Kat held out a spoon full for Shu to taste.

Shu blew on the spoon full of creamed corn and took the bite. "It needs a little more salt."

Kat stirred in some more salt and said, "He's having a hard time with Austin and Marcy's deaths as anyone would. I'm still trying to process the whole thing myself."

"Yeah, I get that. Larry's having trouble with what happened to Austin too. He thought it was unfair, and he feels like he failed him," Ginger described.

"Why do men think they always have to save everyone and then blame themselves when they don't or can't? All this has been way beyond anyone's control," Kat remarked.

"Well, Hugo wants his cake and eat it too. He's had it that way for years. He told me that his wife knows about us, and she's okay with it. I'm her best friend, and now I can't even look her in the eyes once I get home. I broke it off with him," Shu blurted. "Since we were on the subject of men."

"Wow, girl, you okay?" Ginger asked, as she placed her hand on Shu's shoulder.

"Yes, we're talking through the whole thing, but I told him I quit, and we're done. I'll figure something out," Shu answered.

"I'm sorry, Shu. Men can be so clueless!" Kat exclaimed.

"You got that right," Ginger agreed, and they laughed.

"Shh, here they come," Kat announced hearing the door knob twist.

# Chapter 20

They all sat around the cabin eating the creamed corn in the candlelight. Shu observed each of them and wondered what the journey tomorrow would bring. They were still stuck in the middle of nowhere and no closer to home. Marcy lost her life from one stupid mistake, and now Shu wondered who else might not make it out alive. Were they all destined to perish in the crash or will they succumb to their demise in the wilderness? Will any of them make it out alive? It seemed as though they were being picked off one by one and only the strongest would make it home. Was it some greater power's idea of a sick joke or was it truly a predestined plan for them? Could good come out of all of this tragedy? Was Marcy's time up and her number called, or was it just a bad judgement call on her behalf? Death made her head spin since they had been surrounded by it for days. She knew the only thing that kept any of them going was the hunger in their bellies, the drive to survive, and a chance to return to their lives; *home*.

"This is not bad, Ladies. Thanks for fixing it for us," Jesse approved.

"Yeah, thanks," Hugo chimed in.

"Who's getting the pullout bed tonight?" Larry asked, looking at Ginger and smiling.

"The women are sleeping in the bed tonight; you men, can sleep on the floor or in a chair," Shu commanded.

"That's okay with me. I was going to suggest that anyway," Jesse said.

"Oh, alright, but if you all get scared in the night, call me, and I'll crawl in there with you," Larry suggested.

Kat picked up a throw pillow from the couch and tossed it at Larry, "Snake!"

"Easy there, don't be hatin' on me, Kitten," Larry teased.

Jesse couldn't help but chuckle a little from Larry's Kitten crack, knowing he was referring to her Hello Kitty panties. "We won't have a watch tonight, but I'll sleep in front of the door, and it has a pretty good lock on it. I'm sure Jack's long gone by now, at least I hope."

They finished off the creamed corn and found their places for the night. The women lay on the pullout couch, and Henry made himself as comfortable as he could in the old chair in the corner. Larry laid down on the floor next to Ginger's side of the bed and held her hand. Jesse checked the lock on the door and sat down. While leaning against it, he rested his head and closed his eyes.

After about five minutes, "Oh no, I have to pee," Ginger said. She got up and went and stood in front of Jesse, waiting, but he didn't move. He was already asleep. Ginger lightly kicked his foot.

"No, Jacob," he said, waking up and realizing where he was.

"Sorry, I have to pee. Who's Jacob?" Ginger asked.

"My son. Sorry, Jacob used to mess with me when I slept. He got a kick out of torturing his dad. I'll get the door but don't go far, just out of sight. Do you want Kat or Shu to go with you? Larry maybe?"

"No, I'm good. I'll be right back," she said.

"Yes, I'm going with you," Larry insisted.

"Well, come on," she said. They both trotted out of sight.

Jesse closed the door and waited for them to return. Five minutes later, they still weren't back. Five more went by, and he stuck his head out and called, "Larry!" There was no answer. "Ginger!" Still, there was no answer. He turned back into the cabin and said, "I'm going to check. Lock this door and don't open it until one of us comes back." Grabbing his jacket and flashlight, he stepped out.

Hugo jumped up and locked the door behind him. Henry got up and peered out the window, but only saw a forest cloaked in snow.

Kat and Shu sat up, held each other's hand, and worried about Ginger.

After several minutes, *knock, knock, knock* came at the door. "Open up! It's Larry."

Hugo opened the door, and Larry was leaning against the doorjamb with blood trickling down his face from his hairline. "What the heck happened?"

"He's got Ginger. He cracked me over the head with something, and I blacked out."

"Who's got Ginger? Jack?" Hugo asked.

"I assume it was Jack. It could've been Bigfoot for all I know. I didn't really see who it was. When I came to, Jesse was there. He went after them. Man, my head really hurts. I... I..." Larry started to fall. Hugo caught him and helped him into the cabin. Shu and Kat got out of bed and Kat went and locked the door. Hugo sat Larry down on the bed. Shu grabbed the first aid kit and set it down beside Larry. Hugo dug into the kit and retrieved some gauze and pressed it to Larry's wound.

"I have to find her. I have to find her," Larry announced. He slapped Hugo's hand away, got up, and went to the door. "I have to find her!" He grabbed a knife from the sink and unlocked the door, opened it, and ran out.

"Larry!" Hugo called.

He stopped and looked back. Hugo tossed him a flashlight wrapped in a cloth. "For your head, and you might need to see."

"Thanks." Larry turned and ran out of sight.

# Chapter 21

The forest was blanketed in about two inches of snow, and Larry knew he could follow their tracks. He tried to hurry because they had a head start, and he really didn't know how long he had been unconscious. He did know his head still hurt. He touched the rag to his wound, and it stained the cloth red. "Still bleeding," he said to himself. A gunshot rang out in the distance through the quiet darkness and echoed across the terrain, followed by another. He knew he was close. After the sound faded, all that was left was the quiet once again, like it had never even happened.

Larry began to pick up the pace in a panic, thinking that he was too late, and Ginger lay dead against the cold ground after Jack had his way with her. He tripped and fell forward to the ground but caught himself on his hands. He laid there a moment and looked around. He saw a light flashing on and off repeatedly. He peered in that direction and realized it was Jesse, signaling to him. He got up quietly and slowly made his way over to Jesse. "Where is she?"

"He's got her tied up over there about a hundred yards away, hunkered down at the base of large tree," Jesse explained, pointing in the direction they were.

"What are we going to do?" Larry asked.

"He's already taken two shots at me. Maybe we can flank him from each side, distract him, and catch him off guard."

"Okay, which way?"

"You go around that way, and I'll go this way. Keep your light off and be as quiet as possible and as low as possible. If he gets a shot, he'll kill you, or you can just stay here and distract him."

"No, one of us should be able to get to Ginger. Her chances are greater with both of us."

"Okay, slow and low, got it?"

"Got it, Doc, slow and low."

"When I call your name, we'll rush him, and take him by surprise."

They both started to move toward Jack to flank him. They closed the gap about fifty yards, and Larry snapped a twig under his foot. Jack fired off a shot once again, breaking the utter silence through the woods. "I hear you, Doc!" Jack called out and whistled the theme from *The Good, The Bad, and the Ugly.* "You're going to die tonight, Doc! Forget about Red and just leave me be!"

"Don't hurt her!"

"Ah, Larry, you're here too! I've been watching y'all! Sorry, Larry, I got a thang for redheads! This one here's a looker! I'm going to really enjoy her! Mmm, and those freckles!"

"I will kill you if you hurt her!" Larry shouted.

"Larry, Larry, Larry. Don't make promises you can't keep. I promise you, I'm going to hurt her, and she's going to like it. I might even let you watch."

"Why are you doing this?" Jesse bellowed.

Jack jerked toward the sound of Jesse's voice, "What else do I got to do? Jon's dead now, and he kept me from being me, and me want's to play. With him gone, I can play all I want."

"Let her go, and we'll let you go."

"Oh no, Doc, we're not all getting out of this alive. You go, and I'll only kill her, when I'm done copulating and fornicating."

"I can't do that, Jack. I can't let you do that to her. She doesn't deserve this. What? Was your mama a redhead, and she beat you as a child?"

"Doc, I prefer you leave my mama out of this. She didn't like it when I played either."

"What about the Feds? They're looking for you. It won't be long now, and they'll be here. You'll go to prison," Jesse warned.

"It'll be worth it to have my way with this vinegary, rosy peach."

Jesse put his hand to his forehead and knew this man was a vile, perverted, twisted monster. There was no telling how many people he had killed. He knew he was probably going to have to kill him or die trying to free Ginger. There was only one way to do it. He was going to rush him, hoping he or Larry didn't get killed in the process. "Please, Jack! Just let Ginger go, and we'll tell the Feds we never saw you. You can get far away from here."

"You should've seen Austin's face when I knocked him into the river. Oops! Didn't see that coming, did you?" Jack poked at Jesse. "I would've joined your foursome, but I was on the other side of the river."

Jesse didn't respond, but anger boiled up in his chest. He wanted to kill Jack for what he had done to Austin. How could someone kill an innocent boy, a child? This whole time he had blamed himself and all along he was murdered by drowning from Jack's deliberate actions. Jesse motioned with his light to Larry to keep moving closer. Jesse knew Jack only had seven rounds left in his gun, and he needed to get him to shoot some more to lessen his chances of getting shot. Jesse picked up a small fallen log and tossed it in Jack's direction and then took off running away from Jack.

Jack fired off three rounds, trying to hit Jesse, but he couldn't pull a bead on him and missed. Jesse picked up another rotted log piece and chucked it away from him. He began running back toward Jack's direction at an angle, while ducking behind and around trees. Jack fired off two more rounds with one grazing Jesse's side. Jesse fell to the ground and quickly scooted behind a tree.

"Did I get you, Doc? Are we having fun yet?" Jack pricked.

"No, you missed me," Jesse lied. He didn't want to give him the satisfaction of knowing he had grazed him. Jesse checked his wound and saw that it wasn't that bad, just a scratch as the bullet had barely made contact with his flesh. Jesse wasn't sure if Jack had the marshal's extra clip or not, but he knew if he could get to him before he changed it out, he might have a chance.

"Larry! Red's taking her clothes off for me. You wanna watch?"

Ginger screamed through her gag that Jack had tied around her head, as he reached to un-button her slacks. She had her hands tied behind her back and her feet were also tied together. She couldn't do anything but squirm or hop. Jack had her back leaned against a giant oak tree with the front of his body pressed against her and the marshal's pistol in his right hand. When he touched her waist, she twisted and head-butted him in the face and fell down on her side.

Jack shook his head from the stinging in his nose and said, "Oh, you like it rough, do you?"

Ginger was squirming on the ground, trying to inchworm away from him as she feared what he was going to do to her next. He stepped toward her and grabbed her hands and jerked her back to the tree trunk, standing her up for cover. "Try that again, Peach, and I'll pluck out an eye," he said, as he stuck the tip of the gun barrel on her temple and drug it down her cheek and then under her chin.

Ginger could smell his breath on her, and it smelled like tuna and liquor. His eyes were bloodshot and his whiskers were dark and thick stubble. The look in his eyes told her that he was very serious and he could do anything without remorse. His eyes were murky brown and deep, almost black like an onyx with no sparkle in them, soulless. His eyebrows needed a pluck, for they were bushy and full and almost met in the middle. His hair was short and tight to his head like he had had a buzz cut recently. His breathing sped up as he began to rub himself against her again, and the moisture from each breath floated on the air around her. She squeezed her eyes shut, as he reached down for her pants button again.

"Larry!" Jesse shouted, as he readied his pistol and tore off in a hard charge toward Jack and Ginger.

Larry heard Jesse shout, and he tightened his grip on his knife and sprang into ambush mode as he rushed through the woods as fast as his legs and the terrain would allow toward Jack and Ginger.

# Chapter 22

Kat and Hugo just stared at each other fearfully after Hugo closed and locked the door. Shu and Henry were standing and looking at Hugo and Kat anxiously.

"What should we do? Should we go after him?" Kat asked everyone.

"I don't know. He is a grown man and can decide for himself," Hugo responded.

"Yeah, but he's hurt, a head injury," Kat cautioned. "What about Jesse and Ginger? They may need our help."

"Jack has a gun," Hugo declared.

"Well, he can't shoot us all. I'm going to find them," Kat announced.

"I'll go with you," Shu chimed in.

"I'll back you ladies up," Henry offered.

"I guess I'm in too. But if we do this, we need to take some weapons and be able to follow Jesse's lead. He has a gun as well," Hugo agreed.

Kat grabbed a fish filet knife from the cabin's sink. Henry pulled out the knife Jesse had given him. Hugo found a hatchet on the floor by the stove that was used to chop kindling, and Shu reached up and took an antler mount off the wall. She smashed it against the floor breaking the skull plate in half.

"This will work," she said, as she raised it up to eye level, twisted it around, and tested it in her hand with a jabbing motion. Henry, Hugo, and Kat just stood there looking at her as she simulated some kind of Tai Chi moves with the antlers.

"What a wildcat," Hugo whispered to himself with fascination.

"Let's go," Shu insisted.

They walked out into the night in search of tracks to follow. They found several sets that trailed off in the same direction. They followed them with caution, not knowing what they might find at the end of them or if even they would find anything or anyone in the darkness. They heard a couple of gunshots ring out that startled them and caused them to stop, squat down, and scan the area around them. They couldn't see anything or anyone around. The shots were in the distance, and they knew they had to hurry to get to where the shots came from. They continued to follow the tracks as fast as they could without losing them. They stopped and heard voices echoing through the timbers. Then they heard three more bursts of gunshots and then two more as they moved closer to the sounds.

"Some of the footprints separate right here. Jesse and Larry might have split up. Let's follow the pair of tracks that's probably Jack and Ginger's. Ginger's should be the smaller ones," Hugo advised.

They all agreed and followed the pair of tracks, and shortly after, they heard Jesse call out Larry's name. Jesse was very close, and they all began to run toward his voice wielding their weapons and ready to fight for Ginger's life even at the cost of their own.

# Chapter 23

Jack heard Jesse call Larry's name then tromping closer to him. He pushed away from Ginger and scanned the darkness in Larry's direction and then in Jesse's. He readied his pistol, hoping to get a shot at one of them while his heart raced faster. Back and forth, he turned toward the sounds as they got closer and closer. He caught a flash of someone moving through the trees toward him, took aim, and cracked off a round. They fell to the ground and didn't move. He heard something behind him. Just as Jack turned, Jesse tackled him to the ground and Jack dropped his pistol. Jack took a couple punches across the jaw before he landed one to Jesse's cheek, knocking him off of him. He jumped up and grabbed Ginger and pulled a hunting knife from his waist and stuck it to her throat. "Not so fast, Doc. I'll slice and dice Peaches right now. Put the gun down. I know you don't want to kill me, Doc, or you would have shot me already."

"No, I want you to pay for what you've done."

About that time, Hugo, Kat, Shu, and Henry burst on to the scene and surrounded Jack, Ginger, and Jesse. They stopped and surveyed what was going on. Flashlights illuminated the area, and with the help of the white snow, they saw Jack holding a knife to Ginger's throat, while Jesse held his pistol pointed at him. "Jack, I don't want to shoot you. Just let Ginger go. You're surrounded. You have nowhere to go."

"Let her go, Jack," Kat said.

"You don't want to do this, Son," Henry added.

"Oh, but I do, Preacher. I can't help myself," Jack admitted.

"Just put the knife down, and we can talk about it," Henry assured.

"Don't you worry, Preacher Man, I'll spare no details when I confess my sins to you later on. I'm gonna back away, and you're going to let me go, or I'll gut her in front of y'all," Jack threatened.

Out of nowhere, Larry jumped onto Jack's back and grabbed his hand with the knife, bumping Ginger and causing her to fall to the ground. Larry struggled to hang on to Jack's hand, and Jack elbowed him in the face, knocking him off. Jack turned and drew back the knife to stab Larry, but Shu lunged forward with her antlers and plunged them in to Jack's side. Kat sprang forward and sank her fish filet knife deep into Jack's lower back. Henry rushed toward Jack and planted his knife into Jack's shoulder. Hugo leapt ahead and swung his hatchet chopping at Jack's hand that held the knife. Jack fell to ground staining the snow red with his blood.

Larry got up and went to untie Ginger. Henry, Shu, Kat, and Hugo stepped back and looked at Jack lying in the snow in his own blood. They turned to Jesse in amazement at what they had just done. Jesse lowered his pistol, and his jaw dropped at witnessing the onslaught. As they stepped toward Ginger and then closer to Jesse, Shu asked if Ginger was okay. Jesse saw Jack stand back up, and gripping the knife in his back, he pulled it out and grasped for Ginger one last time as Jesse fired two rounds through his heart, sending him to his end.

# Chapter 24

An owl hooted in the distance through the silent night, as they all stood around looking at each other in bewilderment of the last few minute's events. Jack laid face first in the snow again, staining a new area red with his blood. They all encircled Jack's body and stared at him. Jesse wondered what was to come of it. Would the Feds be at the cabin when they got back? Would they be arrested for murder, though it was self-defense? Would this night haunt them for the rest of their lives? They all looked at Ginger, questioning with their eyes did Jack rape her or not. "No, he didn't," Ginger responded to their prying eyes. "I'm okay; just relieved he's no longer a threat to us."

"Me too! That son of—"

"Larry! I'm fine, really I am," Ginger cut him off.

"We are too, glad you're alright," Jesse affirmed, placing his hand on her shoulder.

"Thanks guys, for coming to save me. He was going to kill me after, you know… I'm just so glad you came," she said. "Larry, you're bleeding!"

"My head's fine, but I think he shot me," he responded.

"What! Where?" Ginger called out, feeling around and looking Larry over for a bullet wound and finding blood on his left shoulder.

"Take off your jacket and let me see," Jesse commanded.

Larry removed his jacket, and Jesse assessed his wound, "It looks like a through and through. I don't think any bones were hit. I'll stich you up when we get back to the cabin. You got lucky. Is anyone else hurt?"

"We all got lucky tonight," Hugo claimed.

"I don't believe in luck. Good will always prevail one way or another," Henry concluded.

No one else had been injured in the incident, and no one knew quite what to say to Henry about his comment. They had seen disaster, evil in action, and then they, themselves, had snuffed out a life. Was it really good actually prevailing, Shu thought, or were they all being punished for the way they'd lived their lives?

"Jack killed Austin, he claimed he pushed him in the river, and he'd been watching us," Jesse informed. "Larry, did you hear him when he said that?"

"I did," he responded.

"Holy cow! Are you serious?" Kat exclaimed as everyone shook their heads.

Jesse nodded and said, "Let's get to the cabin. Maybe we can get some real rest now. We'll tell the police what happened here when we get out these woods."

"What, that we all killed a man and left him to rot somewhere in the forest? I don't think we should tell anybody about this. Jack could have just as easy gone missing in the crash," Hugo urged.

"Hugo, we can't do that. We have to tell the authorities where Jon and Jack's bodies are, and what about the other poor man that died at their hands?" Henry reasoned.

"Yea, but we all—How's that going to look for us?" Hugo asked, implying about the way each of them had contributed to Jack's demise.

"It was self-defense, Hugo. They won't press charges for saving Ginger's life and then also Larry's life from a known criminal. Plus, he confessed to killing Austin," Jesse responded.

"I guess you're right. I just never killed anyone before or contributed as far as I know. I'm a little rattled about it," Hugo admitted.

"We all are. Hugo, it will be alright," Shu assured.

"It's never easy taking a life, but sometimes it's necessary to save the innocent or even yourself. And that's what makes it justified in the eyes of the law," Jesse reassured. "Right, Henry?"

"And the Lord's, that's right, Jesse; he would have killed Ginger and maybe even us if we didn't stop him. He was a madman," Henry agreed. "Still, it carries a heavy weight, but we don't have to shoulder any guilt. We're not culpable for Jack's death because we did protect the innocent and that frees us from any guilt. Hugo, you defended Ginger without malice in your heart, and it doesn't make you a killer; it makes you a good Samaritan, which is honorable."

Hugo nodded his head as Henry placed his hand on Hugo's shoulder and squeezed, reassuring him. "Let's get back. Jesse needs to tend to Larry's shoulder," Henry said.

As they walked back, Henry stepped up beside Ginger and asked, "Are you okay? If you need to talk, I'm here."

"I'm okay, Henry. Jack didn't get to do what he intended. Thanks for asking. He didn't hurt me, just scared me," Ginger responded.

"Well, if you change your mind..." Henry offered.

# Chapter 25

The morning sunlight shone through the little cabin window and danced across Jesse's face as the trees swayed in the wind. He had resumed his place on the floor by the front door after patching up Larry's shoulder. He was dreaming of his daughter Paige and the moment when he had said goodbye to her just before she left for Destin, Florida. He had bought her a beach towel with a mermaid on it. She loved mermaids when she was little. Even though she was all grown up, he always saw her as his little girl. He had complete faith in her abilities as an adult, but as a father, he clung to those memories when she was a child and how little girls adored their fathers. After Amanda had passed, they had become even closer than they were when she was alive. They were both very open about their feelings and were real with each other. As a father, Jesse gave her leeway to make her own decisions. Amanda had done a terrific job instilling the proper values in her, and he trusted her.

Paige took the towel and unfolded it, revealing the mermaid scene on it. "Thanks Dad. Remember when you took me to see the mermaid show?" she asked.

"Yes. I thought you were going to dive into the water after them. You were so excited; it was all your mom and I could do to keep you in your seat," he responded. "Sweetie, you know mermaids aren't real," he teased.

"Dad!" she rolled her eyes as they both laughed.

After the show, he had to tell her that day that mermaids were not real. When he told her, it broke her heart so much she cried for the rest day and wouldn't eat. It had become a standing joke between them after the initial shell shock wore off but that didn't stop her from liking mermaids. Even now, she still wore mermaid earrings and necklaces. He smiled as his heart warmed with thoughts of his daughter but then the dream took a turn for the worst. He dreamed that she was getting a tattoo of a mermaid on her back and her boyfriend was the tattoo artist. "No, not a tramp stamp!" he mumbled as he jerked awake.

Jesse rose up and rubbed his eyes and shook off the dream's horror and looked around the cabin. Everyone was asleep, but Kat was sitting up on the floor, leaning against the bed and staring at him. He motioned her to come over. She quietly got up and went and sat down next to him. "How long have you been watching me?" he asked.

"Not long. You were mumbling in your sleep," she responded.

"Yeah, I tend to talk in my sleep a lot. I can't keep a secret. I'll tell it when I'm sleeping," he admitted. "I dream a lot, and I carry on conversations with people in my dreams."

"Who were you just dreaming about?"

"Paige."

"You miss her, don't you?"

"Of course. I have to get used to it though. She's gone off to college now, and it's just me in that big house. Plus, she has a boyfriend, and they seem serious. He may end up being my son-in-law."

"Do you like him?"

"I haven't been around him enough to decide that yet. I know it's silly, but I don't know if there is a man out there that will measure up to my standards for her."

"That's not silly at all. My dad was very protective of me, and no one has measured up to my standards, let alone his," she admitted. "A good man is hard to find."

"She's had boyfriends in the past, but I can tell she's falling for this guy. Did you have a dream?"

"I hardly ever dream, but when I do I can't remember them."

"Consider yourself blessed. I dream almost every night, and sometimes it's very tiresome. It's almost like another life I am living with different worlds colliding together. I have bits and pieces of my life intermingling with strange, and sometimes even disturbing, events taking place all in my head. When I was teenager, I could actually will myself to dream about a specific thing or someone. It's kind of creepy, isn't it?"

"Give me some examples of things or people you've dreamed about."

"Oh, I've had some doozies. I've dreamed I could fly many times. I've dreamed of flying alligators which may have just been dragons, but they looked like alligators with wings. I dreamed I was a pro ball player. What man hasn't, right? I still dream about things that went down in Iraq, you know, people that died. I also dream about my wife sometimes and my kids a lot. Just now before I woke up, Paige was getting a tattoo, which I hope she doesn't."

"Maybe you're just a deep thinker."

"Oh, is that what you're going with?"

"Yep, tattoos aren't so bad. I have a tattoo."

"Yeah, where?" he said, remembering that he didn't notice one on her at the river.

"I can't tell you. Only my future husband will see it, and of course, my doctor."

"Oh okay, lucky him." They both smiled at each other and sat in silence for a while. "I guess we should wake the others and get moving."

"Oh, let them sleep some more. They really need it."

"Ten more minutes and then we'll wake them," he said, noticing how pretty she was even with her disheveled hair. Kat had a natural beauty about her that it didn't matter how she looked or what she wore; even if she had make up on or not, she was still beautiful. *It was a wonder that a man hadn't stolen her away already*, he thought. Her smile was intoxicating to him and her presence made his heart beat faster. He hadn't had that feeling since Amanda died. He wanted to embrace her and kiss her with great affection on her perfectly full-shaped lips. But he was torn in his feelings and knew that this was not the place or the time. They had seen so much lately that he was unsure of her reaction to him. He thought that she was only around him to feel safe, and she was a naturally friendly and curious person. If he landed one on her, she might slap him or lose trust in him. He was having trouble with these thoughts and feelings. He wanted to get out of his own head and just get home. Then he might contact Kat and go on a date or something with her.

"Have you dreamed about me?"

Jesse blushed as his heart sped up, and he felt the flush in his face, "Yes, I have."

"Tell me about it."

"I can't. That's a conversation for another day."

"Oh, lucky you," she said, not knowing he had been thinking of her in that way.

Jesse's face got even redder as he just sat there and smiled, shaking his head. "It's not like that. But you are very pretty, and I did see you almost naked. It's hard to get that image out of my mind, and honestly, I am attracted to you."

"I'm flattered, Jesse Gibson. I am attracted to you as well."

"I was going to wait until we got home but would you like to go out with me sometime?"

"I would like that very much," she said, smiling. She stared at him and noticed how handsome he looked in the morning light with his ruggedness. His hands were strong but gentle, as she remembered him helping her out of the plane seat and their first meeting. He was a caring man with depth in his soul. He knew how to be gentle to a woman and share in her emotions and feel with her. She was captivated by his presence and found herself lost in her thoughts about him. She felt like they were old friends. She was comfortable around him, not intimidated or insecure, but relaxed and could be herself.

"What is it? Do I have something on my face?" he asked, aware of her staring at him.

"No, you're fine, just fine," she said, reaching up and brushing his wavy hair to the right of his forehead.

He could sense the longing between them as they each gazed into each other's eyes. Everything around them vanished away as they both felt that magical moment when they realized that the person in front of them is the one person that can make all of their loneliness disappear. They both leaned in closer to the other in anticipation of that one enchanted first kiss.

Jesse stopped short and whispered, "I'm not that kind of guy."

"I'm not that kind of girl," she whispered back as she planted her lips onto his and the world stopped spinning for just an instant. She knew they both shared in the event that is only experienced once in a relationship. She felt the fireworks, the rockets, explosions, time stopped, and that unexplainable feeling of affection and desire. They both knew in that very moment it was a tiny spark of love that illuminated in their hearts the second their lips had touched.

"Look at that!" Ginger exclaimed as she pointed at Jesse and Kat.

They pulled away and blushed at the surprise of getting caught. "You all need to get up and get ready; we leave in twenty," Jesse said, clearing his throat a time or two and standing up.

"We're not going to talk about the elephant in the room?" Ginger asked.

Kat sat on the floor, grinning from ear to ear as the tingle in her toes continued to surge. Jesse moved around the cabin, unsure of what to do with himself, and then he turned to Ginger and said, "How's Larry's shoulder?" Larry was still on his side with his eyes closed, facing Ginger.

"I see. All business, are you?" Ginger said, looking at Kat as they both exchanged looks with one another. Hugo and Henry looked on without much expression, but Shu was sitting up next to Hugo smiling at Kat.

"What's going on?" Larry rose up and looked at Jesse and then to Ginger.

"Jesse and Kat just kissed," Ginger announced.

"Doc, way to go, buddy. Do we need to give you two some privacy?" Larry blurted and then fell back down to the bed, burying his face in his pillow.

Henry just shook his head and smiled as Jesse gave him a pleading look for a subject change. Jesse finally gave in and said, "Yes, Ginger, we kissed."

"So, are you and Kat like, together now?"

"We discussed going out when we get home. Now, I need to check Larry's shoulder, and you need to get up and get ready to go, please," Jesse concluded with a smile, as Ginger teased with her eyes.

"Okay, whatever you say," Ginger agreed as she threw her pillow at Jesse, and everyone was getting a good chuckle at Jesse's expense.

# Chapter 26

The morning was cool but sunny with snow blanketing the forest floor. Everyone munched on saltine crackers for breakfast that they'd found on a shelf in the cabin. They were a little stale, but they curbed the angry hunger pains that everyone was experiencing from the lack of sustenance. Jesse had taken the other Sig Sauer pistol from Jack and removed the couple of rounds that were left and reloaded them into his pistol clip. He sat Jack's pistol on the table for a moment while he returned his to its holster. He noticed a board in the corner that looked like it had been pried up on in the floor. He squatted down in the corner, removed his knife and pried up the board. "Whoa!"

Everyone was ready to go, and they were just about to walk out the door when Jesse squatted down. They turned to see what he was talking about and watched while he pulled out an AR-15 rifle. He also pulled out a short barrel 12 gauge Mossberg 500 pump shotgun and a 9mm Beretta pistol. "There are several boxes of ammo for each one on the shelves," Jesse added. "I wondered about that ammo just thought the guns weren't here."

"Who was this guy?" Hugo asked.

"I don't know, but hand me a box of those 9mm," Henry said, as he picked up the Beretta.

Everyone just looked at the pistol-packing preacher. "What? We might need them. We can turn them in when we get to the police."

"You ever handled a gun before, Hugo?" Jesse asked.

"I've been to the range a few times. Will those bullets fit in Jack's pistol?"

"No, that's a .357 and these are 9mm," Jesse answered.

"I'm good with guns. I'll take the pump," Ginger affirmed. She looked the shotgun over and opened the chamber by pulling down on the fore stock and then slammed it back up. "If only I would've had this when Jack…" she paused. "Hand me a box of shells, please."

Larry was grinning, watching her handle the gun, "Ginger got a gun. You look gangsta, girl."

"Thanks babe."

Jesse handed her a box of shells and then handed his Sig Sauer pistol and holster to Kat, "I'll take the AR." He removed the extra Sig Sauer clip he had in his pocket and loaded it into Jack's and handed the pistol to Hugo. He checked the magazine on the AR-15, and it was already full, then he slapped it back in. "Load up this ammo and distribute the weight among each of us, and let's get going."

They headed out, leaving the cabin behind and slowly moving through the woods traveling east. The sun glistened off the snow-dusted tree branches, and every once in a while, white flakes would flitter down like it was beginning to snow again. They paired up as they walked: Kat and Jesse, Hugo and Shu, Ginger and Larry, and they spread out several yards apart. But Henry was mixed in the middle, walking alone. "I'm so hungry," Kat declared. "I could go for some pancakes right now, smothered in syrup. Oh and some bacon."

"Yeah, some scrambled eggs would hit the spot right now," Jesse responded.

"With sausage," she added.

"Biscuits and gravy too," he countered.

"How about some French toast?"

"With cheese grits to dip them in."

"A side of cream of wheat."

"Choice of an omelet."

"A bowl of oatmeal."

"Count Chocula."

"Frankenberry," she laughed.

"Fruity Pebbles. We're just torturing ourselves now," he said.

"I know, but it all sounds so yummy. I'm going straight to the Ihop when we get out of these woods, you want to come with?"

"Share a pancake stack?"

"Sorry buddy, you'll have to get your own," she sassed.

"I see how it's going to be, every man for himself."

"Only when it comes to my pancakes."

"Noted," he answered as they smiled at each other.

After about two hours of walking, they stopped for a break to check in with everyone and Jesse wanted to check on Larry. After examining Larry's stitches, he found that they were holding well, and there was no bleeding. "Looks good," he announced. "How does it feel?"

"It's sore, and it hurts to raise my arm," he answered, "but I can move it okay."

Jesses had fashioned an arm sling for him out of some sheet strips from the cabin. "Just keep babying it for a couple of days and then start to move it around more, only if it's not too uncomfortable."

"You got it, Doc," Larry acknowledged.

"Henry, how you holding up?" Jesse asked.

"I'm good. I've been walking five miles a day for over fifteen years, so I'm good to go," he answered. "Just a little hungry."

"How's everyone's water situation?" Jesse asked.

"We have two bottles each," Ginger answered.

"I've got two," Shu affirmed.

"We took all that was left in the cabin, about two bottles each," Kat informed.

"Okay, everyone save at least one bottle for tomorrow in case we don't make it out. Then we need to find another water source," Jesse advised.

Everyone agreed, and after about ten minutes, they resumed walking again. "Hey, you sure you're alright?" Larry asked.

"Yes, I'm fine," Ginger answered.

"Is that shotgun heavy?"

Ginger had her shotgun strapped over her shoulder, "It's not too bad."

"You say you're fine, but are you really? The only reason I ask is my ex-wife would say she's fine but really she wasn't. It was like I was supposed to read her mind or something."

"Larry, I don't expect you to read my mind, and I don't drop hints. I'm really fine. Jack didn't hurt me, and I've dealt with plenty of creeps in my life. He only made me mad, but I'm over it, and I don't have to think about him again."

"So, we're good then?" he asked.

"We are great. What are you going to do when you get out of these woods?"

"I was hoping this redhead I know would take me in since I'm homeless."

"I live with my mom, but I'm sure she'd take you in after she finds out what we've been through. We can play the sympathy card on her."

"Where do you live?"

"We live in a trailer park in Centre Alabama."

"You said that this was your first flight as a flight attendant, right?"

"Yes."

"Why is it then you were flying from New York, since you live in Alabama?"

"The airline had a school there."

"Did you have a place in New York?" he asked.

"No, I have a cousin that moved out there to become famous. I was staying with her while I was in school."

"Did she become famous?"

"Not yet, but she has the drive for it. She designs clothes and wants to be a big name in fashion."

"We could probably afford to rent our own trailer while we figure out our new career paths," he suggested. "I do have a little something set aside for an extreme emergency, and I think this qualifies.

"I'm listening."

"I have a couple of gold coins in a safety deposit box in Stone Mountain that are worth about ten thousand dollars. They were my dad's that I saved for desperate times."

"Larry, you are full of surprises. I'm all in."

"Yeah?"

"Yeah," she boomed, grabbing him and kissing him on the lips.

"Oh my arm, my arm," he said, and then pulled her back close to him with his other arm.

The forest became quiet for a moment. Only the sound of their own footsteps crunching in the snow-covered leaves and an occasional snap of a twig was all they could hear. Hugo had noticed that Shu hadn't really spoken to him much since last night, and he thought he would break the silence. "Shu, I want us to be together."

"I can't. I told you it was over. We are going our separate ways once we get home," she answered.

"I know what you said, but I was hoping you would reconsider your decision. We had a good thing going. We were happy. We still can be, and you love me."

"No, I can't. I'm ashamed and embarrassed. I should've never allowed it to get this far. I do love you, but we... I just can't be with you."

"You were happy, weren't you? We had fun, didn't we?" he asked.

"Yes and yes, but it was at the expense of your wife and my character. Let's just worry about finding our way out of here."

After a couple of more hours, they all stepped out onto a large trail that ran north to south. "This must be an Appalachian trail," Jesse guessed.

"We might be close to a road or even a town," Henry speculated. Everyone got excited at the thought that their long journey was finally going to come to an end, and they all could get something eat.

"Which way should we go?" Ginger asked.

"I think we should keep going east like we agreed. If this is an Appalachian trail, it will run through the mountains, continuing in the woods, and we may miss our chance. What do you all think?" Jesse questioned.

"East, we should go east. Like you said, we are eventually going to walk out of this forest if we stay our course," Henry agreed.

Everyone was in agreement to carry on east like they had planned in hopes of finding a road, a house, or a town. They became anxious as they walked, and thoughts of food and civilization flooded their minds. Memories of home and family, ponderings of their futures with the people they'd met filled them with anticipation. They walked at a faster pace, eager to discover an exit. They seemed to have a purpose, a mission; they were determined to find their way out.

"A road! I see a road!" Jesse exclaimed.

They picked up the pace even more as the road became closer and closer, then Jesse held up his hand and stopped. Everyone halted but Larry, following his lead. Larry kept walking past Jesse. "Whatever happens after this point I want you all to know it has been a privilege knowing each of you."

"Back at you, Doc," Henry blurted.

"Yeah, you too," Hugo added.

The women began to hug like they were leaving each other, and the guys began to shake hands. Once they were done, Jesse asked, "Ready?"

"Let's do this," Kat said as she took Jesse by the hand.

# Chapter 27

"Nothing!" Larry declared as he slumped his shoulders in disappointment looking back at the others, still in the woods.

The rest of them stepped out onto the snow-covered, paved road. They all looked in both directions, and it was just a stretch of empty pavement with forest on both sides. Trees and snow-covered ditches and banks as far as the eye could see until it twisted around a bend. The sky was clear, and the air felt like it was beginning to warm a bit, but the snow wasn't melting. It still had the consistency of powder as the wind blew it off the trees and across the road.

"Which way?" Kat asked.

"There aren't any tracks in the snow. No one has even driven through here," Larry groaned.

Everyone turned and looked at Jesse, "What?" he shrugged.

"You're our leader, which way?" Shu barked.

"I guess we should go south. Atlanta is south," he answered.

They walked for a half hour, and the forest finally opened up into flowing pastures of whites and browns with barbed wire fences running around and through them. Way off the road, they spotted an old farm house down a long, gated driveway. "There!" Hugo exclaimed.

They all got excited about finally finding a house and some semblance of civilization again. They walked up and tried the gate, but it wouldn't open. Jesse hopped up on it and climbed over and found that it was padlocked. "You'll have to climb over. I can't unlock it."

"Ladies first," Henry said, motioning to the gate.

Kat and Shu climbed over together and then Ginger followed handing her shotgun over. Larry climbed over with Henry and Hugo's assistance. Once they were on the other side, they headed toward the house with great anticipation. "I hope they have something to eat. I'm starved," Ginger commented as she carried her shotgun in front of her with both hands.

"Shoulder your weapon, Ginger. We don't want to scare them," Jesse advised.

"Oh yeah, that might look a little intimidating, huh," she answered.

"Yes, since we don't look like hunters. We look like a motley crew of hill people with our dirty and mismatched clothes," he added.

"We do look rough, don't we?" Kat laughed.

"Hey, speak for yourself. I look good, sporting my girl jeans," Larry argued.

"You do, babe," Ginger agreed as she smacked him on his rear.

They all chuckled and continued down the drive. They approached the house but didn't see anyone around. A giant oak tree stood at the right corner of the home with large outstretched branches and a tire swing that hung from the lowest one. The house was a light blue with wide board siding that looked as though it had been painted a hundred times. The front porch was covered and four steps led up to a large deck that sagged a little in the middle. The path in and out was well worn, and there was an old porch swing that hung to the left of the door facing out. "Kat, you and I will go to the door. I think if we all go we might frighten them," Jesse cautioned.

"You're right. We'll stay here," Hugo said as he nodded in agreement.

Kat and Jesse climbed the steps and walked toward the wood-framed screen with the solid white door behind it. "Hold it right there! Don't move a muscle or I'll shoot you!" a voice sounded. Everyone froze. "Now put your guns on the ground."

Jesse slowly removed his AR-15 from over his back and laid it down on the porch. Kat removed her pistol and also laid it on the porch by the AR-15. Hugo, Ginger, and Henry followed suit and laid their guns on the ground in the snow. "We need help, sir. We were in a plane crash miles from here, and we haven't had much to eat in days," Henry pleaded.

"We've been in the woods since Sunday, and help never came. We had to walk out," Jesse added.

"You're not here to rob me?"

"Heaven's no! We just need to use the phone and get something to eat if you can spare it. I'm Reverend Henry Tucker, and these good folks were on the plane with me," he explained.

"Well, I'll be holding onto your guns until you leave. Peanut, get their guns," the voice called. A young girl about twelve ran from around the house and picked up the two pistols. She tucked them into the waistband of her pants and picked up the shotgun. She ran up the stairs and got Kat's pistol and the AR-15. She held them close to her chest, struggling to carry them all.

"Be careful, they're all loaded," Jesse warned.

After she gathered the guns, she ran down the stairs and over to the oak tree, and a big man stepped out from behind the trunk with blood-stained overalls. "Go lock'em in the barn. Make sure you unload them first."

"Yes, Daddy," she said and fast walked behind the house with the guns.

"My name's Jim. Everyone calls me Big Jim," he introduced.

"Are you okay?" Henry asked.

"I'm fine for now," Jim answered. "Some vile men came a couple of nights ago, killed my dog, and shot me. Ava barely got away. They ransacked my house and stole whatever they wanted. They took most of our food, of all things…"

"I'm so sorry to hear that, especially about your dog. Do we need to get you to a hospital?" Henry asked.

"I tried. They have the road into town blocked off. There's only one road in and one road out. I've got no idea why. I checked on my neighbors, but they're gone; they haven't been back. I don't know what the heck's going on. So you say you've all been in the woods since Sunday?" Jim asked.

"That's right," Henry confirmed

"This is Ginger, Larry, Hugo, Shu, and they are Jesse and Kat," he said, pointing to each of them. "Jesse is a medic; he can take a look at your wound."

"Alright, let's get you all something to eat. Come on into the house," Jim said as he limped passed them and up his stairs holding his .30-30 rifle down by his side. Kat and Jesse stepped aside, as Jim opened his screen and swung his front door open. Big Jim stood six-foot six and was a very thick and big-boned man. He had a brown burly-bearded face with kind eyes, and his round belly filled out his overalls. His hands were large, and the one that held the rifle wrapped clean around it. He wore a brown toboggan hat on his head and curly, thick brown hair protruded out from under it. "Excuse the mess. You can have a seat at the table, there."

Everyone kicked the snow off their shoes, wiped their feet on the mat that said *Welcome,* and set their bags by the door. They took a seat at the long table in the kitchen that Jim led them to. He set a basket of biscuits on the table and a jar of honey. "Butter's on the table here," he said, setting down several butter knives, saucers, and spoons. "My daughter made these this morning."

Ginger grabbed the basket first. She removed a biscuit and tore off a piece and shoved it into her mouth. "Mmm, so good," she affirmed, passing the basket.

Everyone else took a biscuit and began to eat, as Jim handed everyone a bottle of water. "Thank you, Jim. Can I please use your phone then I'll look at your wound?" Jesse asked as he stood back up.

"I'm sorry but my landline doesn't work and our cells phones are dead also. The power is out also, both been out since Sunday." Everyone had a disappointed look on their face at Jim's answer. "It must have been some kind of solar storm. It lit up the sky like a colored fireworks show; it's probably what made your plane crash. My SUV wouldn't start after that and those jerks stole my old '73 Ford pickup and my generator. We've been in the dark since Tuesday."

"Where are we? All we know is that we're somewhere half way between Georgia and New York. Our plane went down somewhere in middle," Jesse asked and sat back down.

"You're in Lowesville, Virginia," Jim answered.

Ava stepped through the back door entering the kitchen. She stopped and looked at her dad. "It's alright, Peanut, come on over," Jim motioned.

"I'm Kat. Ava, your biscuits are delicious."

"Thank you. It was my mom's recipe; she made the best biscuits and taught me how."

"Where is your mom?" Kat asked as she looked around the house.

"She's in heaven with Jesus," Ava answered.

Kat's heart sank at her answer, "I'm so sorry."

"It's okay. She passed away three years ago from cancer," Jim explained.

Jesse stood up and interjected, "Let's look at that wound of yours. You want to lay down on the couch or a bed?"

"The couch will be fine." Jim got up and went to the living room, and Ava followed behind him.

Jesse grabbed the first aid kit by the door and walked over to the couch. Jim unclipped his overall straps removed his flannel shirt and then laid down on the couch. He lifted up his t-shirt and long john shirt, exposing the bloody bandage on his side. Jesse peeled back the tape and folded over the gauze. He got whiff of the infection, "This looks bad, Jim. Have you had a fever?" Jesse asked.

"I have had the chills, and I've been aching all over," he answered.

Jesse felt his forehead. "You're burning up with a fever." He pressed around on the wound and some greenish pus oozed out of the bullet hole. Jim's skin around the gunshot was reddened and inflamed. "The bullet is still in there, and it's infected. We've got to get you to a hospital today. If we don't, you will die."

"How long? How long do I have if I can't get there?" Jim asked.

"A day or two tops, maybe less," Jesse warned.

"The nearest hospital is about nine miles away, and we have no transportation and no communication. Can you remove the bullet?" Jim asked.

"I'm not a surgeon. You need antibiotics, an IV, maybe blood, and definitely a skilled surgeon," Jesse answered.

Jim grabbed Jesse by the arm and said, "You've got to try. I can't leave Ava alone. I've got some antibiotics for my cattle."

"Help my daddy!" Ava screeched.

Jesse looked at Ava and then back to Jim, "If the bullet hit an organ, I have nothing to repair it. I can start you on the antibiotics and figure out a way to get you to a hospital. If we can't figure that out then I'll try as a last resort, but no promises. I'm just being real." Jesse cleaned the wound and redressed it with gauze from their first aid kit. "You need to lay here and rest as much as possible. Let us think about this a minute."

Ava went over to her dad and hugged him, "You need anything, Daddy?"

"No, I'm fine. Help these people with whatever they need, okay, Peanut?"

"Okay Daddy, I will," she answered.

"Jesse, you and your friends can get cleaned up and wash some clothes if you need to. We have a large water storage tank, but there's no hot water. You'll have to heat some on the stove and take a bath. But go sparingly; we don't know how long the power is going to be out," Jim offered.

"Thanks Jim, that'll be great."

# Chapter 28

"I checked Jim's SUV over, and its dead in the water. I think the computer is fried. It's not going anywhere; it won't even turn over," Hugo explained.

"We're still stuck, no phone, no car, and no help. There's no way out of here except on foot and now there's more crazy thugs to deal with?" Ginger bellowed. "When's this ride going to be over? I'm telling you if it wasn't for that bath…"

"I know, right!" Kat replied. "It's a good thing we found extra clothes for everyone."

"Well, now we have to find a car to get Jim to a hospital. He's resting now, and I've got him on some antibiotics, but he needs a surgeon or he's going to die. We need to get to a police or fire station to alert the authorities about our crash and what these men have done to Jim and also about Jack," Jesse explained, racking his brain for ideas.

"We're with you until we get to Atlanta. We're a team. Right guys?" Shu asked.

"Whatever it takes, Doc," Larry said.

"That's right, we're with you," Kat answered.

Ava stepped into the kitchen. "Ava, we're going to need those guns back. Kat, will you go with her?" Jesse asked.

"I will," she answered. Kat and Ava walked out the back door to retrieve their guns from the barn.

"We don't know what we're getting into or how many of these men there are," Hugo said.

"We can't hole up here. Jim will die; and the way home is through town. We have guns and ammo if we need them. We'll try to be as stealthy as we can. Jim said it was seven miles to town. We can check with a couple of neighbors on the way to see if someone can help us or has a working car. If we can't get a ride, then we might have to steal back Jim's truck if we can even find it," Jesse explained. "If not, then we pray."

"I'm way ahead of you, Jesse," Henry affirmed.

"I think only a couple of us should go. It might better our chances of getting in and out without being seen," Jesse advised.

"You might need me if we have to work on something," Hugo added.

"You're right. We also might have to borrow a car to hot wire," Jesse agreed. "You know how to do that, right?"

"Are you kidding? That's how I cranked my first car," Hugo bragged.

Kat and Ava came back in, carrying their guns. Ava handed the shotgun to Ginger and pulled out a pistol from her pants and handed it to Henry. Kat handed the AR-15 to Jesse then handed a pistol to Hugo. "We're trying to decide who should go," Jesse admitted.

"I'm going," Kat barked.

"I'm in," Ginger approved.

"Okay, Hugo, Kat, and Ginger, the rest stay here with Jim and Ava. Gear up, we leave in five," Jesse announced.

"You sure you want to go G?" Larry asked.

"Yes, they may need back up. I'll be fine. You stay here and help out with Jim. I'll be back before you know it," Ginger answered and hugged him tight.

"You better come back to me, you promise?" he whispered.

"I promise, we've got a trailer to buy," she whispered back.

Jesse, Kat, Ginger, and Hugo headed out toward town, carrying only their weapons, some ammo, and water. They walked at a fast pace, knowing that they needed to find a vehicle and get back as soon as possible. They knew that they had plenty of obstacles ahead of them even after they found transportation. The snow was finally starting to melt as the temperature rose above freezing and the sun had warmed the ground. They walked for several minutes and spotted a ranch-style home that sat off the road like Jim's. They approached with caution, taking in their surroundings and looking for movement. As they drew near, they noticed the front door was open. "Anyone home!" Jesse shouted as he looked into the house.

No one answered back, and the living room had been ransacked. He motioned for everyone to be quiet and follow him in. He stepped in, and as he passed the couch, he saw a man lying on the floor in a pool of dried blood. He hurried to his side but quickly noticed he had been dead for at least a day or two. He stood up and whispered, "Let's make sure whoever did this is gone."

Room to room, they searched with their guns at the ready to clear it of undesirables and find survivors. They found no one else. Re-entering the kitchen, Ginger picked up the telephone receiver that hung on the wall and checked it for a dial tone. Hugo just looked at her, wondering if she heard anything. "Nothing, it's dead."

"Will you two search for medicine while Hugo and I check the barn for a ride?" Jesse asked. Hugo and Jesse went out the back door and across the yard to a large barn in the back. All they found was hay and an old, broken-down John Deere tractor. Upon returning to the house, they met Kat and Ginger at the back door. "You find anything?" Jesse asked.

"No, they cleaned them out. The medicine cabinet was empty and the kitchen cupboards were bare," Kat answered.

"Nothing useful in the barn either," Jesse acknowledged.

"These guys are killing people for their stuff," Hugo blurted. "Are we equipped to do what's necessary? We may have to kill these guys, if they don't kill us first."

"I don't think we have a choice, Hugo. If it comes to that, we fight, otherwise we get a ride and Jim some help," Jesse answered.

"But we don't even know if we can get past these guys. What if they're a huge gang and have taken over the whole town?" Hugo argued.

"We don't know, but we have to try, and we won't unless we go," Kat broke in. "Besides, we still need food and transportation for ourselves."

"Jim has cattle; we can eat those and stay at his place until this gets sorted out by the authorities," Hugo suggested.

"We don't even know what's going on. We need to get a ride for Jim, and everyone else, and then figure it out as we go. I have a daughter in Florida I'd like to check in with. Hugo, you have a wife and family. You volunteered to come. What's wrong with you?" Jesse asked.

"I don't want to die after facing death twice already. I'm scared, three strikes, you know," he admitted.

"We all are, but that fear is going to keep us alive," Jesse affirmed, placing his hand on Hugo's shoulder. "But I need to know if you can handle it. If you freeze up, it could cost us."

"I won't freeze up; I just don't want to die. I got your back."

"Good, then let's get going," Jesse commanded as he fought with his own fears and uncertainties. Having to take another life was the last thing he wanted to do.

They walked up the road about a mile to the next farm house and saw a newer Ford long wheelbase pickup in the driveway. There was also a nice Lincoln Town car that sat next to it and a giant cutover corn field that ran far back behind the left side of the house. To the right stood a picture-perfect, two-story red barn with an adjoining silo. The home was a brick ranch-style with an attached garage and looked as though it was built in the late 90's. The garage door was closed, and Jesse knocked on the front door then backed up. There was no answer, so he stepped to the window in the door, cupped his hands around his temples, and peered in. He saw the same thing; the house had been ransacked. Furniture was overturned and home decorations were broken and scattered about the floor. He grabbed his AR-15 from his shoulder and alerted the others. He checked the door, and it was unlocked. He turned the knob and slowly opened the door with his rifle at the ready for hostiles. "Let's clear the house," Jesse whispered.

Again, they searched each room, cleared the house, and found no one around dead or alive. Stuff was strewn around the floor and also the kitchen cupboards were bare and all the medicine cabinets were empty with the doors left open. The garage was full of furniture and boxes that had been pillaged through in haste. They all gathered in the kitchen. "What the heck is it with these guys? Food and medicine?" Hugo wondered.

"Maybe they're making drugs," Ginger suggested.

"I don't know; it is a bit odd," Jesse agreed. He spotted keys hanging on the wall next to the back door. He grabbed a set that read *Ford* on them, and he grabbed another. There was a third pair that read *Dodge,* an older set. He handed the keys to Hugo and said, "Try these out with Ginger, and Kat and I will check the barn."

Kat and Jesse went out the back door and headed toward the barn. It had a large sliding door for driving trucks and tractors in and out. Jesse slid the door open, and they entered. There sat an International Harvester combine and a 424D John Deere tractor with a couple of grain wagons. "We can use the tractor and pull one of these grain wagons behind," Jesse suggested.

"That will get Jim there fast, and the bad guys will have no problem catching us," Kat mocked.

"Not for Jim, for us to get to town" he corrected.

"Oh, I thought you wanted us to ride to the hospital like Oliver and Lisa Douglas," she laughed.

"The problem is I don't think we're in Hooterville," he returned.

"I can't believe you got that. You are full of surprises, Mr. Gibson."

"Are you kidding, Green Acres is a classic. Maybe we can catch an episode together sometime."

"It's a date."

Jesse walked deeper into the barn and saw a window off the back and looked out. Several yards away sat an old blue and white Dodge Blue Bird bus that read *Trinity Church* on the side. "Well I know what those old Dodge keys fit. Let's go see if Hugo got us a ride going."

They walked back around the house and to the front, "What's the word?" Jesse asked.

"Same as the SUV, the computers are fried. You find anything?" Hugo asked.

"Yeah, we did," he answered.

"What was it?" Ginger spouted.

"There's a tractor and an old Dodge bus," Jesse revealed.

"Let's give the bus a try. It can't hurt," Hugo claimed.

They all walked around to the back of the barn. Hugo climbed onto the bus, and sat down behind the steering wheel. He pumped the gas, pressed in the clutch, inserted the key into the switch and turned it. The bus cranked over and over, but it didn't start. He pumped the gas two more times and tried it again. Still, it didn't start. He noticed a black knob near the switch. "Ah yes, the choke," he whispered to himself as he pulled it out. He turned the key again, and the engine fired up and burped a puff of white smoke out of the tailpipe. It gained in idle speed as it warmed, and he pushed in the choke and the idle dropped to a steady vibrating chug.

Jesse stood in front of the bus and tapped on the hood, "Check the lights!" he yelled at Hugo.

Kat trotted to the back to check the markers and blinkers. All the lights worked as Hugo went through each one, even the red blinking stop and yield lights. Jesse stepped to the door and asked, "How's the gas?"

"It's full, if you can believe that," Hugo answered.

"Or the gauge is broken," Jesse wondered.

Everyone boarded, and Ginger asked, "Isn't this stealing, like grand theft auto or something?"

"I think it would be a greater crime to let a man die. This is a church bus; therefore it belongs to the people in need of a ride. We'll tell the police we commandeered it to save a man's life," Jesse answered.

"I understand, but what if it's not a church bus? What if this guy just bought it from a church for himself?" she questioned.

"We'll cross that bridge when we come to it. I'll go leave a note," Jesse concluded as he stepped off the bus and ran to the house.

When Jesse returned, Hugo closed the door and dropped the bus into first gear and slowly let out the clutch. The old bus shuddered as he revved the motor, and it jerked into motion as the wheels spun on the wet snow and grass to find traction. They all cheered as the bus rolled passed the house and up the driveway to the road.

# Chapter 29

The bus rolled to a squeaky stop at Jim's gate. Jesse stepped off and ran toward the house to retrieve the gate key. Ava had spotted them, recognized Jesse, and met him half way with the key. "How's your daddy doing?"

"About the same, I guess. He's been sleeping a lot," she responded.

"We borrowed this bus from your neighbor to take him to the hospital," he added.

"Mr. Anderson drives it around, picking up people on Sundays for church. He's my Sunday school teacher. Did he come with you?"

"No, we didn't see him or anyone else. No one was at home. We found the keys and drove it over. You think he'd mind if we borrow it a while? We left a note explaining what we were doing."

"I don't think so, as long as you don't wreck it or nothing."

Jesse smiled and said, "We'll try not to." He unlocked the gate and swung it open and Hugo drove the bus through and up to the house.

Everyone met in the kitchen and waited to hear the next plan while Jesse checked on Jim's condition. Ava watched Ginger and Larry whisper to each other and giggle as they hung on each other. They realized they were being watched by a twelve-year old and settled down. Kat, Hugo, Henry, and Shu discussed the first thing they were going to do when they got home.

"I'm going to…" Kat paused noticing the look on Jesse's face as he entered the room.

"We need to go now. Jim's fever is worse, and he doesn't have much time. He's talking out of his head. I'm sorry, Ava, your daddy's body is not responding to the antibiotics. He's going into septic shock. He needs surgery and fast," Jesse warned. "Pack it up. We leave in five."

Ava teared up, and Kat embraced her and stroked her head. "We're going to do all we can for your dad. Right now, he needs you to get ready to go so he can get surgery. Can you do that for me?"

"Yes, ma'am."

"Okay, get enough clothes for a couple of days. You'll be staying at the hospital with him. Use the bathroom and make sure we have your dad's wallet with his ID or driver's license."

Ava wiped her tears away and hurried off to do as Kat instructed. Everyone else was already packed and ready to go, eager to get going. They had cleaned their guns, reloaded, and filled their pockets with ammo. Kat looked at Jesse and knowing him for the past several days, she had come to recognize certain looks on his face. She knew he was worried about Jim and unsure of his survival because of what they faced ahead. He placed too much weight upon himself, worrying about things he couldn't change. It was one of the many traits she admired about him, his great concern for humanity and human life. Though she didn't know much about his past other than what he'd told her, she felt a deep connection to him. She stood there studying him as he made final adjustments to his pack. She imagined them sitting on the couch together watching TV and laughing while holding each other. She thought of his warm lips and how the world around her stopped spinning when they first kissed. She very much desired to kiss those lips again, again, and again.

Jesse looked over at Kat and seeing her eyes upon him brought comfort. Her gaze had a calming effect on him. Though he didn't know her very well she had a sense of strength that he appreciated. He felt very exposed and vulnerable to her without judgement. His mind raced back to their kiss from this morning. He got a twinge in the pit of his stomach as he relived the moment. He longed to kiss her again but the circumstances demanded other action so he smiled at her and nodded. She stepped close to him, and he felt his heart began to beat faster. *What an effect this woman has on me*, he thought, *the twinge, the elevated heart rate, the longing, the kiss. What is happening to me?* He asked himself. She reached up and placed her hand on the left side of his face and with her thumb she rubbed a spot on his cheek. He wanted to lean into her touch and pull her tight to himself and pretend that they were standing his kitchen alone.

"You had a something on your face," she said as she slid her hand down his neck and across his shoulder after she finished rubbing his cheek.

"Oh, thanks."

"Anytime," she said, smiling as they stood there a minute staring starry-eyed at each other.

Ginger observed what was happening and elbowed Larry in the side and pointed at them. Larry cleared his throat and grunted the words at the same time, "Booty call!"

They both broke their gaze and looked at Larry as Ginger gasped and slapped Larry on the arm. Larry drew back and shrugged his shoulders.

"Load up!" Jesse called. Hugo, Larry, help me get Jim on the bus."

They struggled to get Jim out of the house and onto the bus since he was such a big man. He was unresponsive and delusional from the septic shock. It took great effort, but they finally got him settled into a seat and belted in. Mr. Anderson must have installed seatbelts since buses didn't come equipped with them. Everyone took a place on the old Bluebird, and Hugo fired it up and closed the door. "Here we go," he said, as the Dodge lurched backward and down the driveway through the gate and onto the road. He shifted into first before the bus stopped rolling backward and the gears grinded a bit. "I got this; it's just been a while." They headed toward Lowesville as the sun dropped behind the trees and dusk began to fall upon them.

Several miles down the road, Jim shouted, "Ava! Clara! Clara! Ava!"

Ava rushed to him and said, "I'm here, Daddy. I'm here but Momma's gone. Momma's been gone."

Jesse placed his hand on Jim's forehead and said, "He's on fire; he doesn't have long. Hugo step on it."

They rounded a corner, and the town came into view. No lights were on, just dark buildings were ahead. Hugo spotted a roadblock coming up. Two cars were parked end to end across the road, obstructing the way but no one was in sight. "Uh, Jesse?" he asked as he slowed.

"Can you go around?" Jesse asked.

"I don't think so. The ground looks too soft."

"Go through the middle."

"What middle? There's cars."

"Go through the middle," Jesse instructed as he stood up and said, "Buckle in and prepare for impact. We have to ram through the roadblock." He turned back to Hugo and said, "Just fast enough to move the cars out of our way. Twenty-five miles per hour should do it without hurting anyone."

Hugo maintained a speed of twenty-five mph as they hit the cars with a loud crash and screeching tires. They parted way for them to pass through but not without scraping the sides of the bus, ripping and crinkling metal on all three vehicles. The motor kept running and the Dodge stopped shaking as the last car let go of its grip.

"Is everyone okay?" Jesse asked.

Everyone was fine but bewildered that there was no sign of any people or electricity. They saw cars with windows busted out, hoods up, and doors left open. Glass was strewn across sidewalks where businesses appeared to have been broken into and looted. Debris cluttered the streets and sidewalks along with papers and items from the businesses. As they passed by City Hall, two officers lay dead out front with buzzards picking at their rotting bodies. Some cars had been burned, and some were even turned on their side like a mad mob had moved through with a vengeance. A gun shot rang out and one of the bus windows shattered. Everyone crouched down and scanned the area. A man came running out of nowhere, screaming and shooting. He fired several rounds off, and when the gun was empty of bullets, he threw it at the bus and he fell to the ground and pounded on the dirt as he disappeared from their sight.

"What was that?" Shu shouted.

"I don't know. What's happening?" Henry responded.

"Jim said the hospital is about a half mile passed City Hall. It should be up here on the right, Hugo," Jesse warned.

"There it is," Hugo blurted.

"Is that…It is. He sent us to a veterinary hospital," Jesse disapproved. "Jim! Jim, listen to me! Where's the people hospital?"

"Take care of my Peanut," Jim said as his body went into convulsions. His heart stopped beating and his body went limp.

"Daddy! Daddy!" Ava screamed.

Hugo stopped the bus at the front door of the veterinary office. It looked like it had been looted, and appeared to have been abandoned. Jesse ran inside and grabbed a defibrillator and ran back to Jim. He took out his knife and cut his overall straps along with his shirt exposing his skin. He flipped the switch, rubbed the two paddles together and yelled, "Step back, Ava, don't touch him!" He pressed the paddles to Jim's chest and Jim's body jerked, but there was no response from him. Jesse waited for it to recharge again. He rubbed the paddles together and hit him a second time. Jim's body jerked again, and Jesse felt for a pulse, but there was none. He slumped down, dropped the paddles, and looked at Ava. She threw herself on her dad's body and wept vehemently, knowing he was gone forever.

Jesse stood up and saw everyone looking at him like it was crash day all over again, when people died. Kat grabbed him and embraced him. He was stunned for a second but then embraced her back. "You did everything you could," Kat whispered.

"Yeah, and he still died," he answered.

"It's not your fault, you know that," she assured.

"I know, but it still hurts and now Ava…"

"What do I do now? I'm all alone. I am…" Ava whimpered.

Kat comforted her and said, "You're not alone. We're here. We'll take care of you until we can get you to a grandparent, aunt, or uncle."

"I am alone. My parents were both orphans. I have no other family," she said tearfully.

Kat and Jesse exchanged empathetic looks, and Kat said, "You can stay with us until something changes."

"What do we do now?" Hugo asked. "Do we take Jim back to his place or do we drive on to the next town?"

"It's very clear that something bad happened here. What are we going to find in the next town?" Ginger questioned.

"For real!" Larry echoed. "What the crap is going on?"

"I wish I knew. Since Jim was an orphan, I guess it's up to Ava," Jesse answered.

"Ava, honey, what should we do with your daddy?" Kat asked.

"I want to go home," she moaned.

Hugo turned the bus around and headed back to Jim's. On the way back, they all discussed what could be going on in town, why the police were dead, and the State Police or the National Guard hadn't been called in. "What was that back there?" Shu asked.

"Maybe there is some kind of state emergency going on that we're unaware of," Henry suggested.

"Like what?" Kat questioned.

"Where's all the people?" Larry asked.

"Where was the gang? I'm glad we didn't have to deal with them, but it's just freaky that there were no people, only the one crazy shooter man," Ginger replied.

"Back in the 70's, I saw towns left like that after rioting the Vietnam War. It could be something similar to that," Henry added. "We just don't have enough information."

"You think we're at war?" Kat asked.

"I don't know. It was just a thought, and we've been out of the loop for almost a week," Henry answered.

"The solar storm could have been bigger than just us and this town. Maybe it affected the whole county or a portion of the state," Jesse suggested. "Whatever it is, we need to take care of Jim and get back on the road."


Back at Jim's, Ava clung to her daddy's body as their shadows flickered in the lantern light, and they laid him on a tarp. Kat gently pulled her away, and she buried her face in Kat's chest. They wrapped him up and tied it off with rope. They lowered him into a shallow grave they'd dug for him in the pasture by her mother's memorial site. They knew there were laws concerning burying someone, but they didn't know what else to do. They hoped the county would come out and place him in a casket and vault later on, after order was established again. Ava needed to have closure about her father.

Henry spoke a few words, read some scripture, and closed with a prayer. He seemed like a pro at funerals. He knew exactly what to say, read, and pray to bring solace to those around him. He always concluded that it was not the end, but the beginning to those that had died and with that, hope was planted in the hearts of those listening.

# Chapter 30

They stayed the night at Jim's to give Ava some time to mourn her dad and because they would be sitting ducks to the gang with the bus lights beaming through the darkness. But Jesse made it clear that they were all leaving at first light, including Ava. He didn't feel comfortable leaving a twelve-year-old girl alone to fend for herself. She had just become an orphan and still needed adult supervision. He thought he would deliver her to the police station in the next town. They could contact Child Services to arrange for a guardian and get someone to tend to the animals on her farm. Before they bedded down, they cooked a big batch of biscuits and scrambled eggs to fill their bellies. Ava had collected eggs from the hen laying boxes earlier that day. They took shifts keeping watch to make sure they were not going to be attacked in the night.

A rooster crowed, announcing the coming of a new day, and as the light peeked through the windows, Jesse began to wake everyone. After they all got up and stretched, did their business, and scarfed down the last few biscuits, they loaded the bus once again. Ava's eyes were red and swollen from crying so much. It was hard losing a parent, and she knew it all too well from her mother's death. She also knew what Jesse intended to do with her and was upset but understood. They were mere acquaintances and couldn't take on a girl to raise. They just wanted to get home.

Jesse had found a map of Virginia in one of Jim's kitchen drawers, and they were headed to Amherst which was about twenty miles from Jim's place. They traveled back through Lowesville without incident or seeing anyone stirring. No other cars passed, no people were spotted, and no sounds were heard, just an eerie silence. As they rode through town, they spotted the American flag at half-mast flying at the General Store. They had gotten a second look at the chaos that had taken place and wondered what in the world had happened there. They sat in their seats and gazed in amazement at a town that had been forsaken, abandoned, or simply sieged, but for what reason hung in their minds like a bad taste as they left Lowesville behind them.

Kat grabbed Jesse's hand and squeezed it tight as she turned and looked at him. "I'm glad you're with me. I don't know what I would've done if you weren't on that plane."

"You probably would be squeezing Larry's hand right now," he joked.

She smiled and said, "Maybe."

"What!"

"I knew that would get your goat," she poked back.

"I'm glad you are here with me too, but I wish we would have met when the plane landed in Atlanta and not in some trees."

"That would have been ideal. I feel bad for Ava and having to leave her all alone at a police station," she added.

"I do too, but I don't know what else to do. She's become a ward of the state," he explained.

"We're all trying to get home, and she's basically being ripped away from hers."

"She seems like a strong girl. It will be a major adjustment, but she'll get through it. Who knows, maybe they'll find someone to stay with her at her farm. That way it will still be like home for her. She kind of reminds me of Paige when she was her age with her straight blonde hair always pulled back in a ponytail. Ava's not like other twelve-year-olds. She's more mature and acts like an adult. Losing her mom and working on the farm made her grow up faster," he assured.

"I know she'll get through, it's just—we've bonded," she admitted.

Jesse squeezed her hand and said, "It would be great for her to have a friend like you."

"Jesse!" Hugo shouted.

Jesse got up and went to Hugo's side, "What is it?"

"We're almost out of gas. That shooter must have hit the gas tank yesterday, and it has been slowly leaking out all night. I didn't even notice because it was full when we first drove it," Hugo confessed.

"Okay, well the next car you see on the side of the road stop, and we'll try to siphon some. Hopefully, it will get us to Amherst," Jesse replied. About that time the bus spit and sputtered then the engine went silent. "Coast it as far as you can. Maybe we'll get lucky."

Hugo popped the bus out of gear and let it roll downhill; he braked as they entered a curve which was too sharp for their speed. The curve straightened out and an incline began and the bus slowed. Hugo spotted a dirt road and turned onto it and slowed to a stop. "Well that's that."

Jesse turned to everyone and explained the situation, "We need to find some gasoline. I'm going to walk up this road a bit to see if there is a house with a hose for siphoning. Hugo you work on the hole in the tank. Henry and Shu, you two are on watch. Kat, you're with me. Ginger and Larry assist Hugo in whatever he needs."

Ava peered over her seat, waiting for her instructions and when Jesse didn't give her any, she asked, "What about me?"

"Oh yeah, Ava you have a special project. Kat needs you to carry her backpack so she can be on alert with me. You up for that?" Jesse asked.

"Yes, sir," she answered as she left her seat and headed toward Kat.

Kat smiled at Jesse, and he winked at her, "Let's get going," he said.

The three of them walked up the dirt road, and Jesse and Kat held their guns in their hands just in case. Ava toted Kat's backpack and held the straps in front, glad to have a task to take her mind off her dad. They walked for about ten minutes, and the bus had been out of sight for nine of them. They heard shots in the distance that sounded like automatic rifles. They also heard what sounded like return fire. They stopped in their tracks for half a second. "They're at the bus!" Jesse shouted.

They all took off running back the way they came. Jesse out ran Kat and Ava, and he turned and motioned for them to take cover in the tree line just before the bus came into sight. Jesse charged ahead with his AR-15 raised at the ready, and when he saw the bus with two bodies nearby lying several yards apart, a sense of dread washed over him. He approached with caution, moving his weapon in every direction. He noticed the bus had been showered with bullets, and green antifreeze dripped from underneath. He knew it would never run again. He came closer to the first body, and with great sadness, he saw Shu had been shot in the head. His right eye began to twitch, and they both started to fill with tears. He blinked hard to clear them and refocused his mind. He had been here several times in combat and every time got harder, seeing someone he knew gunned down.

He eased over to the other body, but he had never seen the man before. It was a man in his mid-thirties with long stringy, hair and a full beard, and he was wearing dirty jeans and a camo jacket. He had been shot two times in the chest and the ground was wet with his blood. Jesse stepped into the bus carefully and glanced under the seats and down the rows for anyone. "Clear," he whispered to himself. He then advanced around the bus only to find Henry sitting in the dirt with his face in his hands, weeping. Jesse squatted down next to him and asked, "Are you shot?" Henry shook his head. "What happened here, Henry?" When Henry looked up, Jesse saw a small gash in his cheek and it was swollen.

"I heard a truck coming, so I handed my pistol to Shu and told her, Ginger, and Larry to go hide in the woods on the other side of the bus. Hugo was under the bus, and I didn't have time to tell him to hide. There were five men in an old, beat-up Chevy pickup truck; two rode in the front and three in the back. They were armed with AK's and AR's. They rode up on us quick. I tried to talk to them, but they weren't giving any information about themselves. They seemed annoyed and in a hurry. They saw Hugo come from underneath the bus and asked him if he was a mechanic or knew how to work on cars. Of course, Hugo answered yes. They asked me what I did for a living or if I had a trade. I told them I was preacher and would be happy to pray with them. That's when one of them hit me in the face with the butt of his rifle, and they all laughed about it," he answered.

"What happened to Shu?"

"They were going to take Hugo, but Shu came running up and shot one of them in the chest and then another shot her," he answered.

"Did they take him?"

"Yes, they took him. They left me and said they had no need for a preacher."

"Where are Ginger and Larry?" Jesse asked.

"They haven't come out of the woods yet. They probably think I'm dead too."

Jesse heard a twig snap, and he swung his AR-15 around and aimed it in the direction of the sound.

"Whoa, Doc! It's just us," Larry said surprised.

Jesse dropped his rifle and turned back to Henry, "Do you think they'll come back?"

"Maybe, I think they're patrolling for people to capture. I heard one of them say that they needed a doctor," Henry answered.

"We need to get off the road and travel through the woods. Which way did they go?" Jesse asked.

"Toward Amherst," Larry answered.

Jesse stepped back around the bus and whistled for Kat and Ava to come out. They appeared from the trees and stepped onto the dirt road. They trotted up to Jesse. Kat was looking around him. "It's Shu. She's gone," he said.

"Oh no! Shu..." Kat said as tears welled up in her eyes.

"They took Hugo. They took him because he knew how to work on cars," Jesse explained. "Everyone else is okay, except they assaulted Henry. Hit him the face."

Kat leaned into Jesse, and he hugged her. Ava leaned onto Kat and hugged her also. Ginger, Larry, and Henry came from around the bus, and Ginger hugged Kat. The men placed Shu's body on the bus and closed it up. Henry said a few words as he shook with sorrow and wept through them. "Evil is at our threshold, but you, God, hold the keys to the door," he whispered as they turned and stepped into the woods.

# Chapter 31

They walked along the side of the road under the cover of the tree line and waited for Jesse to give an 'all clear' when there was no cover for them. He was on point, and he looked, listened, and waited before giving the signal for them to proceed. Once they reached Amherst, they had no choice but to walk down the pavement. Several cars were on their sides. Some sat like they had broken down, and some had been pushed out of the way. Still, there were no people, no movement; it was like they had stepped into an episode of the *Twilight Zone*. Even though it was a weekday and also midmorning, no businesses were open; no lights appeared to be on anywhere and the town seemed deserted. It was just like Lowesville, debris scattered around, and businesses had been looted.

Ginger stopped walking in the middle of the road and looked around as she studied her environment. "Did we not get the memo? Did we miss the evacuation? Did we go through a time warp? Look at this place, it's deserted, a ghost town. Where's all the people? Are we in danger? Was there an Ebola outbreak? I'm freaking out here, people!" she exclaimed.

Everyone was tired from the morning's adrenaline rush and still in shock over Shu's death. They stopped and just stared at her not knowing what to say. They were all thinking the same things, why were they the only ones around except for the goons that shot up their bus? What has happened in the state of Virginia to cause people to disappear or vacate?

"I don't know, G," Larry answered. "But we're here; I'm here, all of us together."

"Minus two!" she bit back, "or three or four if you count Marcy and Austin."

"Yes, that was unfortunate, but let's figure it out," he agreed.

"Unfortunate! Shu was murdered. That's not 'unfortunate'. That's awful! It's horrible, horrendous, and just evil! She didn't die from an accident, a wound, or a sickness. She was *murdered,* Larry! It's not 'unfortunate'," Kat barked.

"Easy, Kitten, that's not what I meant. It was awful, and I'm sorry she was murdered. I was just trying to help G. It came out wrong, okay?" he admitted.

Jesse touched Kat's arm and said, "Hey, look at me."

Kat slowly turned and looked at Jesse, "I'm just sad about all of this," she answered.

"It's a lot, I know, a little unbelievable even," he understood.

"But we're here living it," Ava affirmed. Their hearts sank as she spoke those all too true words.

"Jesse, listen!" Ginger said.

"It's the truck! That's the one. It's coming!" Henry warned.

"Kat, take my rifle and give me your pistol," Jesse commanded. They quickly swapped weapons. "Quick! Behind that car!" he exclaimed, pointing to a Suburban across the street. They all ran to hide where Jesse pointed, and he just leaned against a streetlight close to where they were standing.

Kat ducked behind the car next to Henry and then noticed that Jesse didn't follow. She rose up and yelled, "Jesse! What are you doing?"

"We need the truck! Stay hidden and stay ready!" he answered.

"What is he doing? He's going to get himself killed," Henry stated.

"He said be ready," Kat affirmed. "Ginger, be ready to shoot."

Ginger positioned her shotgun and clicked the safety off. Kat laid down under the car and positioned the AR-15 in Jesse's direction but not directly at him. The truck rode up to Jesse and stopped several feet away. This time there were only two men in the truck. Jesse kept his head down with one foot propped up on the pole like he was taking it easy. The driver was a middle aged white man with a ball cap on that read *Peter Built*. He shut the engine off and said, "Hey! What are you doing?"

Jesse kept his head down and didn't answer. "Hey you! Poop stain!" the driver yelled and flicked a lit cigarette butt at him. Again, Jesse didn't look up as the butt landed beside his foot still smoldering. "Go slap this moron and see what he's doing here," he commanded the passenger. The passenger opened his door, stepped out, and proceeded to come around the truck. Jesse grabbed Kat's pistol from behind tucked in his waist band, swung it up, and fired off a round, hitting the passenger in the upper chest area and dropping him to the ground. He fired off another into the shoulder of the driver and ran to the truck ready to fire another. The man struggled, fumbling around to find his pistol. Jesse smacked him in the face, opened the door, and drug him out. He fell to the pavement and yelled, "My shoulder! You shot me, you Jerk Wad!"

Kat rushed over with the AR-15 at the ready and checked on the other guy. He was still alive, and Kat kicked his gun away from him. He wasn't going to make any sudden movements by the looks of him. Larry and Ginger came over also, but Henry kept Ava back. "You have something of ours," Jesse said.

"What's that?" he asked, grimacing from pain.

"You took one of our people; Hugo is his name. He was working on our bus before you riddled it with bullets. We want him back," Jesse declared.

The man started laughing and said, "You want…We want…You don't get what you want without Junior saying you can have it." He laughed even louder, "You're going to die and your women, they're going to wish they were dead."

Jesse pressed on his bullet wound, and he screamed and shook with pain. "I'm not joking. You killed our friend and took another.

Where is he? You're going to tell me, or you're going to wish *you* were dead."

The man whimpered and said, "Okay, okay. The high school up the road, he's there with all the others."

"What others?" Jesse asked.

"The whole town, at least all the ones that stayed behind," he answered.

"Where did the rest go?" Jesse asked.

"You don't know?" he laughed again. "You don't know."

"Know what?" Ginger pointed her shotgun at the man.

"The apocalypse, Honey," he grinned at her, baring his nasty tar-stained teeth.

"Kat, is that guy still alive?" Jesse asked.

"Yes, but he's losing a lot of blood," she answered.

"Henry, the first aid kit," Jesse called.

Henry and Ava walked over and handed Jesse the kit. He went around to the first guy he shot, drug him over close to the driver and checked him over. "Good, the bullet exited." He took the AR-15 from Kat and ejected a round out of the chamber. He picked up the round and pressed the pointed copper tip down on the pavement at an angle, pushed firmly and broke it free from the brass. He cut open the man's clothes, with scissors from the first aid kit exposing the bullet hole in his chest, and then sprinkled gun powder in the wound. "This is going to hurt like crap, but you probably deserve it," he said as he lit the powder on fire. The man convulsed with pain, screamed, and then passed out. Jesse rolled him over and did the same to the exit wound. They all watched, dazed at what Jesse did to the man's wound. "You're next, big boy," Jesse warned as he sprinkled the driver's bloody bullet hole with gun powder and clicked on his lighter.

"Wait! Just wait a minute now. What's that going to do for me?" the man asked.

"It's going to stop the bleeding," Jesse answered.

"But the bullet might still be in there," he pleaded.

"Oh, it is. But by the time you wake up, we'll be gone, and you won't bleed to death. At least you'll live, unlike our friend," Jesse explained.

"I didn't kill that woman. I just drove the truck. Junior will kill me if I don't do what he says. He's not a very stable-minded person," he confessed.

"Tell me what you mean by 'the apocalypse'," Jesse insisted.

They all paid close attention to what he said next. "This is the house that Junior built. This is the malt that lay in the house that Junior built. This is the rat that ate the malt—" Jesse lit the powder, and the man yelled with anger and agony then passed out.

"What the…" Larry questioned.

"It's a Mother Goose nursery rhyme, *This is the House that Jack Built*," Jesse said, cutting him off. "He was taunting us."

"What do you think he meant by 'the apocalypse'?" Kat asked.

"I don't know, but it can't be good by the looks of Lowesville and here," Jesse answered. He checked the fuel gauge in the truck. "We've got about half a tank of gas. Let's find the police station, get Hugo back, and get out of Dodge."

Jesse picked up the AK-47 the man had dropped when he was shot and handed it to Henry. He also picked up the Glock 19 from the seat of the truck that the driver had almost pulled on him and handed it to Larry. "Don't shoot yourself or any of us." He wiped some blood out of the seat and sat down in the truck behind the steering wheel. Kat and Ava removed their packs, set them in the back, and got into the front. Henry, Ginger, and Larry climbed into the bed and sat down. They drove slowly down the road closer to downtown and spotted a McDonalds ahead across Main Street. They proceeded to the McDonalds to see if they could find something to eat. The windows had been busted out of the restaurant's front door, and they found no food inside, not even condiments.

They drove back up to Main Street and turned by the post office and located the police station. They pulled into the parking lot and ran inside. There was no one around, no dispatchers, no officers, and no clerks. It was vacant like the rest of the town. They noticed that the gun locker had been emptied and the door left open. Ginger checked the drawers on the only two desks in the building and found a couple of packs of peanut butter crackers, a Ho Ho snack cake, and a small pair of binoculars. Kat picked up a phone receiver from one of the desks and listened for a dial tone. There was none, so she returned it to its place. "I don't know why I thought—there's no power," she said.

"What now?" Ginger asked as she plopped down at the desk beside Kat and peered through the binoculars.

Kat stroked her own hair and said, "I guess we go to the high school."

Ginger tossed Kat a pack of crackers and said, "Well, I hope they have some decent food to eat."

"Does this mean I get to stay with you?" Ava asked Kat.

"Yes, you get to stay with us," Kat answered and motioned for her to come over. Ava walked over, and Kat hugged her tight.

"I'm sorry about your friend," Ava said.

"I'm sorry about your dad and having to leave your home. We have each other now and Jesse," Kat assured.

"What about me, Kitten? You got me," Larry offered. Ginger threw the Ho Ho and hit him in the chest. He caught it and smiled, "It's mine now."

"Larry, I'm sorry about earlier, about losing my cool," Kat admitted.

"It's all good, Kitten. I feel your pain," he acknowledged.

Jesse and Henry studied the map of Amherst hanging on the wall and found that the high school was only about a mile and a half down Main Street. Jesse looked around and found a map of Amherst County and shoved it into his back pocket. "Let's see if we can find Hugo," Jesse said. They loaded back up and drove out of the police station toward the high school.

# Chapter 32

Jesse pulled the truck into a driveway near the high school and up to the house, leaving it running. "See if anyone's home," he said through the rear sliding window to those in the back. Larry and Ginger hopped over the side of the bed and trotted to the front door. They noticed the door was not shut and pushed it open.

"Hello! Is anybody home?" Ginger called. No one answered, so she turned and looked at Jesse and shook her head no. Jesse motioned for them to follow as he pulled the truck behind the house to conceal it from the road parking it behind a patch of trees and thicket.

They got out of the truck, Jesse pointed, and he said, "By my calculations, the high school should be through that patch of woods there. Henry, I would like for you to stay here with Ava and the truck. If you hear me shoot, bam, bam, bam and a short pause and bam again come find us as quickly as possible in the truck. It may be our only escape."

"I can do that," Henry agreed.

"Kat, Ginger, and Larry, let's do some recon first to see what we're up against. Larry, you need a quick lesson on handling that Glock?" Jesse asked.

"Nah, G showed me how it works," Larry answered.

"Okay, then let's do this," Jesse prompted.

They walked into the woods, and about three minutes later, the high school campus came into view through the trees. There was a putrid smell floating in the air as they came closer to the school. They came to the edge of the wood line just before a baseball field and a storage building. They scanned the landscape to get the lay of the land. Ginger had her binoculars out, looking, and she quickly took a step back when something came into view that startled her. She pointed in the direction of what she saw and handed the binoculars to Jesse. He looked out across the other ball field, and tucked down by the practice field and a few small trees, he saw what had startled her. It was a pile of dead bodies, a dozen or so, and that's where the smell seemed to be coming from. "Bodies," he gasped. Jesse handed the binoculars to Kat, but she didn't want to look. "You know we're going to have to check those for Hugo."

"I was afraid you were going to say that," Kat groaned.

"Looks like the forest goes all the way around the two fields. It should conceal us enough to make our way around unseen," Jesse suggested.

They made their way around the ball fields by the cover of the trees and came closer to the pile of bodies as the stench grew stronger. Larry started to gag; he stumbled and fell, landing only inches away from a corpse that was covered in maggots. He gagged even more. It was a young girl, a teen maybe; she had been shot in the head and was half naked. Larry drew back on his knees and noticed several more young girls lay slain in the woods, their bodies decaying. No doubt these girls were raped and tortured and made to do things that no one should ever be made to do. They were so young and had their whole lives ahead of them but were snuffed out by some crazed psychopathic nut jobs. There was not just a dozen bodies in the pile they'd first spotted. There had to be at least twenty-five or thirty bodies of men, women, and even some children scattered out across the little patch of trees beyond the pile.

Their hearts sank, and Kat and Ginger began to cry. Jesse's stomach immediately became queasy at the thought of one these girls being his own daughter. Even though they were someone's daughters, the thought of his own hit harder than expected. He wondered where Paige was and what she was doing. Was she safe? Was she looking for him? When he spotted the children that had been killed, tears welled up in his eyes. The scene was grim, even more than that of the plane crash. These people were slaughtered. "What kind of mad men can do this?" Jesse asked.

"Monsters," Kat answered, composing herself. "These are not men; they are barbarians, and they need to die."

A twig snapped behind them, and Jesse twisted around with his AR-15, and Ginger spun around with her shotgun. A coyote stood with its head lowered, tugging on one of the bodies for his mid-day snack. Jesse charged the animal, running it off for now, but it would return for a feast later. "Let's check the rest for Hugo as fast as we can."

Larry pulled his shirt up over his nose as he and Ginger began looking at each body for a familiar face. Kat and Jesse helped to check the deceased under the concealment of the thicket and only the pile was left to search. "You guys keep watch as Kat and I go check," Jesse announced.

Kat and Jesse low-crawled slowly to the pile of bodies and began looking at each one since almost all of them in the pile were men. They gagged as the stench of rotten flesh and the working of maggots assaulted their senses. They had to roll them over to get a look at those that lay under each one. They tried to move slowly and meticulously so as not to bring notice to the pile if someone was looking in their direction. When they finally laid eyes on the last one, they let out a breath of relief that they're friend might still be alive. They slowly made their way back to cover with Larry and Ginger.

"He wasn't there," Kat informed.

"Oh, thank God!" Ginger sighed.

"That means we have to go in," Larry revealed.

"That's right, as quietly and as stealthily as we can," Jesse agreed.

They all eased back around the fields within the tree line to the school buildings. It was a layout of several brick buildings of one-

and two-story add-ons that had been built over several decades as the county had grown in population. They surveyed the front of the campus; it was a long parking lot with a few cars that sat parked. There were no people in sight, and no gun-wielding thugs. It was unnervingly quiet and still.

They went back to the end of one of the buildings and checked a door, but it was locked. They checked another on an adjacent building, and it was unlocked. Kat opened it slowly, and Jesse peeked in. It was just a long, empty, dark hallway. Jesse stepped in and cautiously moved through the hall with Kat, Ginger, and Larry behind, checking each class room as they passed by them. Student's artwork of pencil sketches and paintings lined the walls and a hint of paint and new carpet smell hung in the air.

After searching the building's bottom floor, they climbed the stairs to get a better view and to search it as well. The decor changed from art to architecture, and the paint smell faded but the new carpet scent stayed present. They proceeded to the next building and the next; classroom by classroom, they searched.

"I need a potty break," Ginger suggested.

"Yeah, me too," Kat agreed.

"Are y'all kidding me right now?" Jesse asked.

"I could go," Larry added.

"Right here, but ladies first. Please remember to be as quiet as you can," Jesse said and pointed toward the girl's bathroom. They went in as Jesse and Larry stood outside on watch. A door opened down the hall and a man stepped through with an AK-47. Jesse pushed Larry back into the opening of the girl's bathroom and motioned for him to be quiet. "Let the girls know someone is approaching," he whispered.

Larry stepped up to a closed stall where he saw Ginger's feet and whispered, "Someone's coming down the hall, shhh."

The man strolled closer as Jesse readied himself to surprise him. He stopped several feet away from the bathroom and stuffed a pinch of snuff in his lip and then spat against the wall. He wiped his mouth, grunted, and then started to walk again. When Jesse saw one of the man's feet come into view, he stepped out and hit him with the butt of his AR-15. The man fell to the floor on all fours, choking on his fresh dip of snuff. Jesse kicked the AK-47 out of his reach and pointed his rifle at the man and said, "Where are you holding the people? The hostages?"

The man spat out blood and tobacco as he tried to regain his wits then sat back against the wall. "You just screwed the pooch, mister," he answered, checking his face for cuts.

"I've seen your carnage out back. You and your buds will get the death penalty for sure, and it's well-deserved," Jesse accused.

"Who are you and what rock have you been under?" he laughed as Larry, Kat, and Ginger stepped out of the bathroom. "There's no death penalty. There's no law anymore, you Puke. Oh, who do we have here? Ladies, ladies...I'll give you and you're friend there a fifteen minute head start, but you're leaving this one," he said, nodding to Jesse. "If I were you, I would take me up on my offer. Junior loves using up sweet little things like you two... In fact, if he keeps going, there won't be any sweet little things left for me. Maybe I'll keep you all for myself. Tick tock, ladies, tick tock."

Ginger handed her shotgun to Kat and squatted down close to the man, "Fifteen minutes, huh?"

"For you, Red, I'll make it an even twenty," he answered, looking her over with lust in his eyes.

Ginger punched the man in the mouth and said, "You're an animal. I'm going to give you five minutes to answer my friend's questions, and if you don't, I'm going to shoot your manhood off with my 12 gauge."

He shook his head, rubbed his mouth, looked at Kat then back to Ginger and offered, "Oh Sugar and Spice, I like it rough, but that's a little too rough. What do you say you all just leave here, and we'll act like this never happened."

Ginger took her shotgun from Kat and poked the barrel into the man's junk and applied some pressure and warned, "Four minutes."

He squirmed and planted his hands on the floor and made a little adjustment with his hips, "Honey, I think you're serious," he said as his eyes widened.

"Let's try this again. Where are you holding the people?" Jesse asked.

"In the gym. They're all in the gym, except a few are in the shop working on cars," the man answered, losing his false bravado.

"Where's the shop?" Jesse asked. The man gave directions to the shop, explaining that it was through the gym.

"How many henchmen does this Junior have here?"

"There's ten of us."

"Do you or Junior, or any of his men, have a working vehicle?"

"We have an old Chevy pickup, a '57 Chevy, and some kind of other beat up jalopy. They're working to get more running in the shop."

"What happened here? How did Junior come to be in power?" Jesse asked.

The hall door opened again, and a man stepped through. He saw his buddy on the floor and opened fire on them. They ducked back into the bathroom and a stray bullet hit the man in the leg. "Oh! You idiot! You shot me!" he shouted.

"Sorry, Fred!" the newcomer said as he paused his firing.

Ginger stepped out and fired off two rounds into the man with a gun, sending him to his demise. Fred scooted and reached for his rifle when Ginger pumped a third round into the chamber and said, "Don't do it!"

He grabbed the gun and fumbled to get it into position when Jesse fired off a round, killing him. "We need to move!" he said, picking up the dead men's weapons. "We just announced ourselves."

Larry slowly walked passed the man Ginger shot, studying his wounds and whispered to himself, "I don't think I ever want to tick G off."

# Chapter 33

Henry and Ava watched as Jesse, Kat, Larry, and Ginger disappeared into the woods. Henry walked back to the truck, popped the hood, and opened it. The old, rusty hinges creaked as they stretched out. Henry stared down at the 283 V8 engine, wondering if he would see any of those V8 engines again. Ava stepped up beside him, and he looked at her. She touched his hand and said, "You're worried about them, aren't you? It's gonna be okay."

"I know it is. You're a strong girl, Ava. We find ourselves in the strangest of times," he responded.

"Whatcha looking at?" she asked.

"Well, I was going to check the oil, but I was just trying to take my mind off things for a minute." He reached down and pulled out the dipstick and turned away from the truck to see the oil level. "Looks good, clean and clear; must've been changed recently." He returned it to its tube and pushed it back in place. He reached up and placed both hands on the front of the hood and said, "Watch yourself," then slammed it down. Some time passed as they both just piddled around, observing the ground and the trees around them.

"How old are you?" she asked, breaking the long silence.

"Old as dirt. Do you know how old dirt is?" he answered, leaning against the truck.

She smiled and said, "Ancient."

"That's right, I'm ancient."

"You're twelve, right?"

"Yes, sir."

"What grade are you in?"

"Seventh, and we're on Christmas break."

Henry thought about that for a moment and what had happened to them over the last five days. Sadness washed over him when he realized this would be her first Christmas without her dad. He thought of his wife and longed to be with her again. Then he thought of Bianca and stated, "I've got a granddaughter about fourteen. She plays basketball for her school. Do you play a sport?"

"No, since Momma died, there's just not time with the farm and all. Daddy kept me pretty busy, working."

"A little work never hurt anybody."

Ava's facial expression changed from mild to pained, "That's what Daddy always used to say."

"Ava, I'm sorry. I didn't mean to…" Henry grabbed Ava by the arm and pulled her around the truck and made her duck down with him. The sound of an engine roared slowly by from a red and white '57 Chevy. Two men occupied the front seat, and the two in the back were the ones that Jesse had shot for the truck. The trunk was open and piled with stuff, probably stolen goods from the residents of Amherst. Henry peered around the pickup to watch them and see if they were going to be a threat or not. He reached for his pistol, checking to make sure it was still there.

Ava didn't know what he was doing until she saw the car. She paid no attention to the noise from the motor. "Do they see us?" she asked.

"No, I don't think so," he answered in a low voice. Some muffled gunshots rang out in the distance. They just stared at each other; fear entered their minds as the car rolled on by out of sight. "Those were gunshots, but it wasn't the signal." Two more shots sounded, but they were different than the others. They were shorter bursts, then one final shot. Silence invaded their ears as they concentrated on listening for Jesse's signal, but it never came. He wondered if their friends were dead, and if they should go anyway to try to find them.

"What should we do?" Ava asked unsure.

"We wait, listen, and have faith that they're going to be alright as you said they would be. Okay?" Henry said, nodding his head.

"You're right. They're going to be okay, like I said," Ava agreed, trying to convince herself.

# Chapter 34

Kat checked the hallway through the classroom door window. "All clear," she said to the others as she opened the door and stepped out. The others followed her as they crossed the hall to another classroom and checked the front of the school from an upstairs window. "Jesse, look," she announced.

Jesse hurried to see two more thugs exiting a '57 Chevy, plus the two he had shot and left earlier. "I knew I should've tied them up somewhere. They'll be able to recognize us and want revenge."

"There was four less men to deal with, now there's plus two. That's eight guys against the four of us; and they have machine guns. We need to cut the head off the snake, Junior being the head," Larry asserted.

"You're right, Larry, we do. But we're going to have to go through his men to get to him. I hate to say it, but we need to shoot to kill. Anyone with a gun, take them out. Are you all okay with that?" Jesse asked.

"I am," Ginger spoke up first. "After seeing what they did to those people out there, yeah, I'm okay with that."

"Larry, Kat?" he questioned.

"We've got to do what we've got to do," Larry said. "Kill the Snake King, right?"

"Right. How's your shoulder by the way?" Jesse asked.

"It's better, still sore, and it's still a bullet hole in me. Let's try not to get any more today."

"Copy that. Kat?"

"I'm with you. These men need to pay for what they've done; we'll be saving more lives in the process. It's not going to be easy, but I think it's the only way," she agreed.

"What do you think about splitting up into pairs? We might have a better chance of taking these guys out if we do," Jesse suggested.

"I don't really like it, but you may have a point. If we do, we might be able to get the jump on them," Kat admitted.

"Oh man! You're killing me. Split up? Today is the first day I've even held a gun," Larry complained.

"You can do this, Larry. I believe in you. You came after me when Jack had me. You dove into that river after Austin. You wore that unicorn shirt. You put on those girl jeans," Ginger encouraged.

"That unicorn shirt was the worst, and hey, you know I rocked those jeans," he bragged. "Fine! I'll do it, but I want one of those machine guns."

"We can make that happen," Jesse offered.

"We need a few minutes, Jesse, you know, just in case…" Ginger nodded toward Larry.

Jesse raised his eyebrows not sure of what she meant by that. Was it to teach Larry how to use the AK-47 or for a pep talk? Surely, she can't actually be talking about having sex? His thoughts steered clear of any thoughts that had to do with Larry being naked. He shook his head and then said, "Whatever you need."

Ginger drug Larry to a corner of the room and showed him how to properly operate the AK-47. Jesse watched them, and he was relieved, thinking that he was way off base about what she meant.

"How do you know all this?" Larry asked.

"I had a stepdad for a while, and he sold guns for a living. He had a shooting range in his gun shop. It was one of my favorite past times, shooting, I mean. He taught me how to shoot, handle guns, and we even hunted a little together."

"Wow! You never cease to amaze me, girl," he added.

"I know. I'm the woman of your dreams."

"You are." He kissed her on the lips and squeezed her to him with the rifle between them.

"Cool your jets, mister. Save it for the victory," she smiled mischievously and kissed him again.

"What happened to him, your stepdad?"

"My mom screwed it up, like she always does. He was a good guy, like Jesse."

"I knew it! I knew something did happen on that river bank with Doc."

"Whatever!" she rolled her eyes and kissed him again. "You be careful and don't get shot again."

"I don't plan on it. That goes for you too, the not getting shot part." They both got real serious looks on their faces, and then they embraced and held each other. "I think I'm falling for you, G." Larry whispered.

"I told you I was the woman of your dreams. I'm falling for you too, Larry."

Kat and Jesse stepped back away from the window after checking it again. "I hope this is the right decision. What if we don't make it?" Jesse asked.

"Don't second guess yourself, not now. Junior still has hostages, and he still has Hugo. They killed Shu and all those people out there. We have a better chance this way, and I know you know it or you wouldn't have suggested it," Kat urged.

"You're right. It's just... I don't want anything to happen to you, or Ginger or Larry or Hugo. No more innocent blood spilled," he admitted.

"I don't want anything to happen to you or us either," she agreed and grabbed his hand and intertwined her fingers with his. "You promised me a movie night, and I expect you to deliver."

"And I'll do my very best."

"See that you do, Mr. Gibson."

He looked deep into her eyes and got that feeling in the pit of his stomach again, "You're a remarkable woman, Katy West."

"That's what you tell all the ladies," she smiled and gazed back into his eyes.

He leaned in close to her and whispered, "You are so captivating." He kissed her on the left cheek and said, "You are very impressive." He moved to the other side and kissed her on the right cheek, "Enchanting even." He looked her straight in the eyes with their noses touching, "So beautiful." Then he kissed her on the lips with gentle passion and a rush of emotion brought tears to her eyes.

When the kiss ended, she spoke in a low whispery voice, "Whoa! Mr. Gibson, I believe you have stolen my heart."

"And you mine, Ms. West, and you mine." They embraced tightly and pondered what all this meant for them with the outcome of this day.

When each couple had finished their tender moments, they came together and discussed which direction each pair would go. They took an inventory of their ammo and checked their weapons. Jesse gave Kat the other AK-47 to go along with her pistol. Ginger had her shotgun, and Jesse had a pistol and his AR-15. Kat and Ginger hugged and wished each other well, hoping that they would meet again. Jesse and Larry shook hands, and Larry said, "Doc, watch your six. Isn't that what they say?"

Jesse nodded, "Yes, you watch yours and hers."

Ginger wrapped her arms around Jesse and said, "Thank you for all you've done. I don't think I've thanked you yet."

"Don't get all sentimental on me, you've got this," he responded. "And you're very welcome."

Kat hugged Larry, keeping distance between them, but he pulled her close into him. She relaxed into his embrace, thinking it was genuine but he made a purring sound and said, "Meow."

Kat pushed him away quickly, shook her head, and pointed her finger at him. She turned to Ginger and asked, "Can I shoot him?"

Larry held up his hands, "Retract the claws, Kitten, just trying to lighten the mood."

Ginger poked Larry in the side and said, "He's harmless. He just has a prickly exterior shell."

"Are we good? You know where you're going?" Jesse asked, breaking up the commotion. "Remember, make your shots count. I'm sure they have way more ammo than us. We're dealing with murderers, rapists, and psychopaths, so don't get caught."

"We're good, got it," Ginger answered and Larry agreed.

"Then let's do this," Jesse said, checking to make sure the hallway was clear.

# Chapter 35

Ginger and Larry took the stairs to the first floor and continued to clear each classroom as they went. They couldn't leave any rooms unchecked in case there were hostiles lurking. They left one building and entered another. "G, this school is huge. Those killers could be anywhere."

"That's why we have to sweep it on our way to the gym, so we don't get ambushed from behind," she answered. "Who knows, we might get lucky and find some food along the way. I'm starving!"

"You're always hungry," he said.

"My mom always said I had a tapeworm, but my doctor said I have a fast metabolism, and I need to eat a lot to keep up with it."

They stopped in a small classroom and noticed that cabinets hung on the back wall. Ginger looked around, and hanging on the walls were posters about cooking, parenting, and sewing. "Home Economics, this is Home Ec. Check those cabinets for food," she demanded.

"I didn't know they still taught Home Ec," he commented as he opened a cabinet door then another in search of some hidden morsel of food. "Cleaned out, empty. Maybe they don't teach Home Ec."

"Well, a girl can hope."

They were continuing their sweep through the building when they saw someone walking in the adjacent building, and it wasn't Kat or Jesse. They hid and watched an overweight, bald man open a vending snack machine with a key and remove a bag of chips. He opened the bag and proceeded to eat them. He stood there and consumed the entire bag, closed the machine door, but didn't lock it and walked on in the direction of the gymnasium and out of sight.

"Let's go get some of those chips," Ginger asserted. "I don't think he locked it back."     They hurried over to the other building and to the machine. Ginger pulled on the door, and it swung open. Her eyes lit up at the sight of goodies, and her belly gave a growl at the anticipation of something to fill it. She and Larry grabbed the snacks and filled their pockets. When there was no place to put any more, Ginger ripped into a bag of chips and chewed in delight at the taste. Larry found an oatmeal pie and gobbled it down, realizing how hungry he really was.

They heard a noise down the hall, and they ducked behind a corner waiting to see what it was. The overweight, bald man came strolling back up the hall. He saw the door to the vending machine open and some other snacks lying on the floor. He drew his pistol and hugged the wall and moved toward them. "I know you're there, come out, and I won't tell Junior."

Larry was leaning against the wall with his rifle up and his finger on the trigger. He turned and looked at Ginger. She nodded, acknowledging she was ready to make a move. Larry stepped out and shot the man in the stomach while Ginger went low and shot him in the legs. The man fired a round, and it ricocheted off the wall by Larry's head. The man fell down, gasping for air and then suddenly stopped moving. He was dead. Larry just stood there and stared at him, shocked. Ginger tugged on his jacket and said, "Let's go."

They both ran out of the building into a courtyard area to return to the adjacent building they were in earlier. They saw two more men running toward them with guns. The men fired several rounds at them. Ginger blasted off two shots, and the men took cover behind some brick flower islands and benches. Ginger and Larry re-entered the same building and ran down the hall to another corner, stopped, and took ready positions to defend themselves. Ginger pushed two rounds into her shotgun, pumped it, and pushed in another. "Are you hit? Are you okay?" she asked.

"No, I'm good. You?"

"Yeah, I'm okay. That was close."

They watched as the two men approached the glass doors at the entrance of the building. The men were wearing camo just like the ones at the bus. Larry pointed his AK-47 and squeezed the trigger hard, firing off three consecutive rounds, shattering the glass, and hitting one of them in the upper thigh. The man that was shot fell down and the other ran off. The man pointed his rifle at the building and emptied the magazine and cursed as bits of mortar and brick flew all around Ginger and Larry as they hunkered down to avoid getting hit.

When the last shot rang out, the man tried scooting away from the door. Larry and Ginger both came crunching through the bits of debris and glass and dispatched the man with a single shot.

"The other guy got away. Wow! My ears are ringing," Larry affirmed.

"We know where he is going and that was very loud."

"That's four. Six more and this is over."

"That's if that guy was telling us the truth, which I hope he was. Plus, we know two more are wounded," she added as she brushed the dust off of herself and shook her hair out.

# Chapter 36

Jesse stepped down a dim hallway with his pistol at the ready and Kat right behind, checking their rear with hers. Their rifles hung over their backs with the barrels pointing toward the floor and could be swung up and accessed at any moment. They seemed to make a great team. They could anticipate each other's moves. Kat was comfortable handling her weapons and Jesse appeared to have a lot of experience in these urban combat situations. It made sense, since he was a military medic. Classroom by classroom, they checked each one for hostiles. The hall wall had a giant mural painted on it with a knight wearing a maroon cape, holding a lance and sitting on a white horse with the heading that read *Amherst Lancers*. No doubt it was the high school mascot.

The next room was the front office, and they entered with caution. Papers and office supplies were scattered all over the floor throughout. It was like someone had been searching for something. Kat couldn't help herself and picked up the phone receiver and listened. There was still no dial tone, and she laid it on the counter leaving it off the hook. It was like she was almost mad at the phone for not making a sound.

Jesse entered the principal's office and read the name on the wooden desk plate that lay on the floor, Albert Goossens. His office was tossed and the file cabinets had been gone through. His desk drawers were left open, and a picture of him and his family hung on the wall above the mess. "Somebody was looking for something," he commented.

Kat poked her head in and said, "I'd say they were. The phone is still not working." She stepped to the front counter and squatted down, pulled back a curtain that covered the miscellaneous clutter of office supplies, a Lost and Found box, and a plethora of brochures and printed notices. She shifted some items around and found a small block of fruit cake that had been left behind. She unwrapped it and gave it a sniff, shrugged, and took a bite.

Jesse stepped up next to her to see what she was doing, and she offered him some. He took a bite and was surprised by the agreeable taste. He looked around at the room and saw a cluster of eight by ten photos of the founders and main staff hanging on the wall. He stepped over to them and read some of the names in tiny print under the portraits. He noticed Albert Goossens hung there among them. He was a balding man, probably in his late fifties if not older. He wore a bushy, black mustache with thick eyebrows to match.

Gunshots rang out nearby. Kat and Jesse turned and looked at each other, paused, and listened. It fell silent again for several minutes then it sounded like a war had broken out. Rapid fire followed by a single shot and then it was quiet once again. "Do you think they're okay?" Kat asked.

"I sure hope so. Let's keep going." They left the main office and proceeded in the direction of the gymnasium to complete their mission. Once out of the building, they holstered their pistols and pulled their rifles up at the ready. They could see the side entrance to the gym, and no one else in sight. No guards were posted outside, but chains and a padlock prevented them from entering. They scanned each direction and kept moving toward the doors. Once there, Jesse tugged on the chain and said, "We can shoot it and maybe it will open."

"That will announce our presence," she advised.

"Yeah, I know. But I'm sure they already know we're coming by now." They went around the building to try to find another entrance and found another door also chained and locked. "We either bust through the front, or we shoot one these locks. What do you think?" he asked.

"I think it's suicide. We don't know what's in there or how many. As soon as we shoot, they'll be right on us. If we try the front..." she paused when she saw a red dot show up on Jesse's heart and then one on hers.

"Busted!" a voice sounded from above.

They froze and slowly looked up and saw two men on the roof with rifles drawn down on them. Two more came from behind, and the one on the roof spoke again, "You have nowhere to go, and you're dead if you make a move. Lay your guns and knives down and put your hands on your head."

Kat and Jesse had no choice but to comply, and they slowly laid their weapons on the ground and placed their hands on their heads as instructed.

"That's a good boy and girl. Junior wants to see you," the man said. After about a minute, the man came around the building and motioned for them to come toward him. One of the other men from behind pushed Jesse and laughed as the other picked up their weapons. "That's it, come on, you can do it."

They rounded the building and arrived at the front entrance. The man opened the door and led the way into the darkened room that was illuminated by the opening. Kat gasped at what she saw. It was mostly men mixed with a few teen boys and some kids that lined the walls with bed rolls. Two guards stood at each end with automatic rifles. Some of the captives looked dirty and sweaty like they had been working outside. There must have been at least fifty people in that gymnasium. The bleachers were folded up against the wall, and the smell of sour body odor and sweat penetrated their nasal cavities. The men took them down four steps into the boy's locker room and around some rows of lockers and pushed them down onto their knees.

"Well, well, well," a deep, gruff voice spoke from out of the coach's office. Out stepped a man in full camo with a brown winter vest on. He was a tall man, in his early thirties and about six-foot two. He was clean shaven with blue eyes and short, sandy blond hair that was parted to one side. His build was muscular, and he spoke with authority. He smiled. "I wanted to get a look at who has been killing my men. I am Junior, and you owe me a debt for each one you've killed and injured."

# Chapter 37

"You see, when someone takes something from me, I have to take something from them. Is this your wife?" Junior asked, pointing at Kat

Jesse shook his head without speaking. He studied his surroundings, counting men, weapons, and exits, and in his mind, he tried to form some kind of counter attack plan for escape. He thought they didn't have much of a chance if he and Kat were separated. They would probably do to Kat what they had done to those young girls out in the woods. They had come so far, and he was not going to let some deranged madman stop them now.

"No? That's too bad. She's a good-looking woman," Junior continued. "Where did you come from and why are you shooting up my school? Are you Feds?"

"No, we were in a plane crash on Sunday in the mountains, and we've been trying to get some help," Jesse responded.

"Help! I'm sorry, buddy, but help isn't coming. You hear that, boys? These two were in a plane crash and need our help," he joked. The other men standing around chuckled a little. "How many more of you are there?"

"It's just us," Jesse answered, hoping they didn't know about Ginger and Larry.

"You see, that right there is a lie. You're starting off our relationship with lies. You know my wife lied to me once. She said she wasn't having an affair, but I caught her. I followed her one evening and took photos of her in bed with another man. She told me she had to work late. While I drained the blood from her veins, I showed her the photos. You know what she said then? 'I'm sorry! I'm sorry!' 'I'm sorry' doesn't change the fact that she let some other scab violate what was mine. You may not have pulled the trigger, but those men your friends killed were mine."

A man stepped up and kicked Jesse in the stomach, and it took his breath away. "I'm going to ask your girlfriend here one more time, and if she doesn't tell me the truth, I'm going to take off one of her fingers." Another man stepped up and handed Junior a scissor cigar cutter.

"Two. There's two more of us," Kat blurted.

"But I haven't asked you yet," Junior corrected. He leaned over to two of his men and whispered to them and then said aloud, "Go find them and bring them to me."

Jesse looked at Kat as he caught up with his breathing. She gave him a look and motioned with her eyes. Jesse looked in the direction she hinted as Junior spoke to his men. He saw a pile of old worn-out football pads several feet away. He looked at Kat again and questioned with his eyes, and she motioned again. *What was she talking about*, he thought. He studied the pile of pads, and lying on the floor poking out from under a thigh guard was the end of a broken broom handle. *Is that what she wanted me to see*, he wondered.

"It won't be long now and your friends will be with you. There's an order of things around here. Everyone works for me and does what I say or they die," Junior explained as the two men left the locker room to hunt for Ginger and Larry.

"Who put you in charge?" Jesse asked.

"I did, and the only reason you're still alive is because you *owe* me. But your girlfriend here, she will help pay off some of that debt tonight when I take her into my bed."

"Over my dead body!" Kat exclaimed.

"That can be arranged, Darling. It makes no difference to me."

Jesse and Kat exchanged looks again, but Kat had a more worried look on her face. Jesse knew he had to do something and soon. This guy was a stone-cold killer and had no conscience. Kat was quiet after that, not wanting to provoke the monster. Jesse studied Junior's other two henchmen to see how they handled their guns. He tried to see if their safeties were off, and if their fingers were on the trigger. He calculated the distance between them and him. His mind continued to race for a plan of attack. Each scenario he went over ended in the loss of his or Kat's life. He could deal with one or two men, but three was game over. He noticed that Junior was unarmed, but he did have a hunting knife on his belt that was in a closed sheath. If he took on Junior, the two other men would shoot him or Kat. If he jumped one of the men, the other would shoot him or Kat. He needed a distraction or one of the men to leave.

They heard gun fire in the distance. "Maybe sooner than we think," Junior smiled. The gun fire got closer to the gym then it sounded like it was right outside the building. A haunting silence fell as everyone waited for the men to come to the locker room with their new captives, but no one came. "Go check!" Junior commanded one of the men.

The man left the room, and Jesse started running his scenarios again in his mind. His odds just got better. "Does it make you feel like a big man to enslave all these people?"

"Actually, it does. I feel very powerful. When I control a person, it gives me a warm, fuzzy feeling, right here," Junior answered, pointing to his heart.

"Did your wife control you?" Jesse asked, trying to get a rise out of him for a distraction.

Junior rushed over to him and bent over to his eye level. "You don't know who you're dealing with. I'm—"

"Believe me, I know," Jesse cut him off and then head butted him in the nose. He drew back and punched Junior in the throat, stood up, and pushed him into the man with the gun. The man stumbled back into a row of lockers. Blood spewed from Junior's nose as he gagged and choked, struggling to get a good breath of air. Jesse grabbed hold of the man's rifle and tried to remove it from his hands, but the strap was around him. The man kicked at Jesse as he tried to rid himself of his attacker. Jesse took the kicks and then with one hand on the rifle he reached for the man's knife, pulled it from its scabbard and pushed Junior aside. Jesse tried to stab the man, but the man blocked him and managed to land a forearm into Jesse's cheek.

It took Kat a second or two to figure out what just happened, and she stretched out and grabbed the broken broom handle. It was about two and a half feet long with a jagged stake-like break at one end and a rounded smooth edge at the other. She squeezed the handle tight in her hand and rushed to help Jesse.

Junior was clutching his throat as blood and drool ran out of his mouth. His eyes were beginning to clear from the water that filled them due to the blow to his nose. He grabbed Jesse by the arm, and Kat swatted him across the back of the thigh as hard as she could swing. He grunted and stepped back and turned toward her. She smacked him across the face with the stick and the cartilage in his nose burst through the skin. His eyes filled again as he tripped over his own feet and landed face first into the floor and didn't move.

Jesse swung at the man with the knife and sliced open his arm. The man let out a yelp. Jesse swung again, cutting the man's ear. Kat stabbed the man in the leg with the wooden handle, jolting him enough that Jesse plunged the knife into the man's chest, causing him to release his hold on Jesse and his rifle. He fell back onto his butt as he slowly slapped at the knife with a bewildered stare on his face. They both stood there and watched the man's life quickly ebb away.

Kat turned to look at Junior, but he was gone. "Where did he go?" she asked as she heard the back door to the locker room slam.

Jesse cut the strap on the man's rifle and checked the clip, chamber, and safety. He pulled the man's pistol from its holster and handed it to Kat. "I don't know for sure, but I felt his hyoid bone crush when I punched him in the throat. He probably won't be able to breath or swallow well. He can't get far."

They heard some gun shots in the gym, and they positioned themselves to take out those that came down the steps, one on each side. They started hearing a lot of voices and then some cheers. "What in the world?" Kat questioned.

"I don't know but be ready. It could be some more of Junior's men," Jesse whispered. He drew a tight bead on the top step and waited for someone to come into view. Finally after a minute, he saw a foot and then a leg slowly approaching. He applied a little pressure to the trigger, moving it a millimeter and tightening it up. He saw another set of feet and legs. His mind raced with anticipation and his heart pounded in his chest with a rush of adrenaline. He waited for his kill shot opportunity. Feet, legs, gun, torso, and then the head appeared. He started to pull the trigger and realized the face was familiar. "Larry?" he whispered to himself. "Wait! Larry is that you?" Kat looked at Jesse, eager to know.

"Jesse?" Larry answered.

"Yeah, it's me and Kat. Are you safe? Is Ginger with you?"

"G's right here, and we got the bad guys. We're clear up here. Are you down there?"

Jesse stepped out at the bottom of the steps and saw Ginger and Larry standing there. "We're clear, but Junior slipped away from us."

Kat and Ginger rushed and hugged each other. "Oh, thank God! I was so worried when I heard the shots," Kat admitted.

"We had a couple of close calls, but we managed. You would've been so proud of Larry," Ginger said.

Jesse stepped up to Larry, and they shook hands. "I didn't think I'd ever say it, but I'm glad to see you, bro."

"Me too, Doc."

Jesse turned and saw men approaching from behind Larry and swung his rifle up. "Whoa, Doc, it's okay," Larry announced, pushing his barrel down.

Jesse noticed a familiar face standing there. He realized it was Albert Goosens, the principal from the photos. "Mr. Goosens, please shed some light on this situation."

"Do I know you, sir?" Albert asked.

"No, I saw your name and picture on the wall in your office," Jesse answered.

"Ah yes, my office," he said. "Well Mr....?"

"Jesse."

"Well, Jesse, after the National Guard left, Junior invaded our town with his hooligans. He robbed and shot people, killed a bunch, ran off a bunch, and took over the high school as his 'Ground Zero', as he called it."

"Where are the police?" Kat asked. Albert turned and looked at Kat. "I'm Kat by the way."

"It's nice to meet you, Kat. The police here were killed by Junior and his men. The state police never came or were never even called, as far as I know. The solar storm wiped out all communication," Albert explained.

"Is the whole state out of power?" Kat asked.

"Where did you all come from?" he asked.

"We were in a plane crash on Sunday in the mountains several miles on the northeast side of Lowesville. Once we got out of the woods, it was like the world had gone crazy, people killing people, cars aren't working, the power is out, and no phones are working," Jesse described.

"It's not just the state that's out of power; it is the whole country. The solar storm was very severe. It hit the west the worst. It caused meteor showers in the pacific that created tsunamis up and down the coast. The National Guard said that California was totally gone, completely wiped out, no survivors. It fell off into the ocean, they claimed. The surges of water stretched as far as Texas, Utah, and Idaho once California dropped off. Half of Mexico is gone along with parts of Nevada, Oregon, and Washington. It's been one of the darkest weeks of our nation," Albert explained.

Jesse was trying to process the information as he watched Ginger and Kat begin to cry. "How do you know all this, and where did the National Guard go?"

"The president sent military messengers to many of the National Guard units in several close states and cities. Amherst was on the list. Several old deuce and a half trucks and trailers showed up Monday morning and loaded up people with supplies for those in need in the west. They filled us in on what had happened and half the town went to help. As soon as they left, Junior swooped in on us, and we've not heard anything since."

Jesse's stomach felt sick as the news of so many lives lost began to sink in. He felt weak, dizzy, and doubled over in anguish from the horrible news. Tears assaulted his eyes as he quickly rubbed them away, and he thought of Junior still on the loose. "Junior got away, but he's hurt."

"All of his men are dead," Larry claimed.

"He's a coward. He'll run until he finds more men to follow him and his twisted way of thinking. John, Steve, go down and get some guns and go hunt that demon down," Albert commanded two men standing close by.

"On it with pleasure," John said as he and Steve trotted down the steps.

"We had a friend with us. His name is Hugo, and Junior's thugs took him from us this morning. He may have had him working on some cars. Have you seen him?" Jesse asked.

"Come with me." Albert motioned to the four of them as he gave more instructions to set the women free from the girl's locker room. They followed him through some doors and a short hallway that led to the auto shop. There in the bay sat an old, flatbed truck with several bodies on it covered by a tarp. Jesse pulled back the tarp and among the dead was Hugo. He'd been shot in the head. "I'm sorry about your friend. He was not going to help them, so they shot him."

"They killed his girlfriend back on the road. I guess he figured…" Jesse didn't finish his sentence, shook his head, and then covered him back up.

"What now?" Ginger asked.

"Henry!" Jesse exclaimed. He stepped out of the shop door and fired off his signal into the air that he had set with Henry. "He'll be coming to the front."

"We'll go meet him and fill him in," Ginger said as she tugged on Larry's sleeve.

"Are you sure you want us to do that?" Larry asked.

"No, just fill him in on Junior and Hugo but not about the country. Let him get settled some first, and I'll tell him. He's going to be devastated," Jesse admitted.

Jesse and Kat met a lot of the town's people as the women were reunited with the men and some wept at finding out that their loved ones had been killed and even worse, raped. Ginger and Larry led Ava and Henry into the gym and filled them in on what had transpired. Henry went right into preacher mode and began to comfort others and offered prayer for those that had lost people. Jesse sat down on the floor against the bleachers and let out a big sigh as he scratched his chin through the whiskers on his face. Kat sat down next to him, wrapping one of her arms around his and laid her head on his shoulder. She began to cry again, and she leaned over and buried her face in Jesse's chest. He tried to comfort her as sorrow swept over him like a wave from the loss of so many lives. It was hard news to accept. California was gone and some thirty-nine million people were swallowed up by the dark, angry waters of the Pacific. He thought, this disaster will echo across the land for decades and maybe even centuries if the nation lasts that long. When Jesse finally told Henry about the west, Henry covered his face with his hands and blubbered like a child. "The Lord has cast judgment upon our nation, heaping up the dead. The Lord giveth and the Lord taketh away," Henry whimpered.

# Chapter 38

The morning air was dry, crisp, and cool. The sun shone brightly in the sky with a couple of small, white clouds slowly drifting to the east. All the snow had completely melted and disappeared, and the birds chirped all around. Larry plopped a twenty-four pack of water onto the tailgate of the old Chevy truck and slid it toward Ginger as she arranged other supplies close to the cab. Jesse worked on strapping a five gallon can of gasoline to the side with some ratchet straps. Ava was stacking food into a box that Albert and some others had given them from Junior's huge accumulation. Kat took an inventory of ammo for each of their guns and wrote it down for Jesse to review when she was done. Albert brought her plenty more for the road just in case they ran into Junior or more like him. Junior had been busy collecting it from all the citizens of Amherst and Lowesville. He had quite the stock room of guns, knives, and ammo in the assistant coach's office.

"Do you think they'll get the power back on soon?" Ginger asked.

"By what Kat and I read about solar storms up in the library this morning, it could be a while," Jesse answered, and Kat nodded in agreement.

"How long's a while, Doc?" Larry questioned.

"It could be a year or several. They might get a small portion of an area powered up but even that will take months. Of course, generators will work if you can get the fuel, but without power, you can't pump it."

"Almost all electronics are affected by solar storms, and with the magnitude of the one we had even other countries may have been affected as well," Kat explained.

"That means the banks are all shut down. No one will be able to get to their money without the internet since most everything is digital now. No wifi, no credit card or debit card purchases, no phone service, no GPS, oh man, no Ebay!" Larry ranted. "Crap! And no TV! There goes my Netflix subscription. Wow, it just keeps getting better. With the cars and trucks not running either means the food deliveries have stopped. Food will be scarce now. People will be getting desperate like Junior. Are you sure we don't want to just stay here?" Larry urged.

"You're welcome to stay as long as you like. You all have certainly earned a place in our community," Albert offered. "With so many gone and deceased, I'm sure we could find you a nice place to reside."

"I have to find my daughter, or otherwise I might take you up on it," Jesse responded. "Don't forget that Ava has plenty of cattle on her farm. They'll need tending to. When things get back to normal, if they ever do, we'll come back and put the place up for sale."

"We've locked everything up. Here are the keys if you need anything. There are chickens, goats, and feed in the barn. We have twenty-five head and two milkers. I'm sure they need milking right now," Ava explained.

"I'll send someone out today," Albert assured.

"I'm going to stay here for a little while, to help these people mourn and move forward," Henry announced.

"Henry, what about your wife?" Kat asked.

Henry took Kat by the hand and squeezed it, "We've always served the Lord and tried to fill a need. Right now these people are in need. My wife will understand and would probably want me to stay, because she would do the same. She'll be well taken care of by my two sons. I'll get back home soon. Maybe they can get a car running for me in a couple of weeks."

Kat pulled him into a hug and squeezed him tight, "Thank you for all you've done for us."

"It was my pleasure. You will be in my prayers regularly," he said as they broke the embrace.

Jesse reached out his hand, and Henry shook it and then they hugged as well. "Are you sure? There's safety in numbers."

"I'm sure. I know the Lord wants me to stay."

"I guess I can't argue with that. Stay safe, my friend."

"You too," Henry nodded.

"I found this U.S. road map in one of the cars in the parking lot. I'm sure it will be helpful," Albert said and handed it to Jesse.

"Thanks." Jesse opened it up to Virginia and began to study it. "I think we should stay away from the interstates. They're probably jammed up with broken-down vehicles.

"That's probably a good call," Albert agreed.

"Looks like U.S. 29 to Greensboro, North Carolina, and then we'll reevaluate."

"It's about two and a half hours to Greensboro. That's if you can go the speed limit. With stalled cars, you may run into issues; you'll have to be careful. There are probably not many running cars out there, so someone might try to take yours," Albert warned.

"Copy that," Jesse agreed.

Larry slammed the tailgate shut with the last of the supplies being loaded. Ginger took a seat on the floor of the bed, and Larry climbed in and sat down next to her. She secured her shotgun for easy access between some boxes. He leaned against the side and propped his arms on the top of the bedside. "Let's get this party rolling, Doc."

Jesse looked at Larry and nodded, shook Albert's, hand and climbed in behind the wheel. Kat opened the passenger door and slid into the seat and into the middle. Ava got in and slammed the door shut. Jesse cranked up the engine, and the truck revved high until Jesse tapped the gas. The motor dropped down to a low grumble as the body of the truck shook back and forth to the stroke of each piston. "You'll take care of Hugo and Shu?"

"You have my word. We'll give them a proper burial," Albert assured.

"Godspeed, until we meet again," Henry said as he tapped the truck twice, letting them know it was clear to go.

Jesse pulled off and up the school drive as everyone waved, and they turned onto U.S. Route 29 headed south. It was just patches of woods and pastures of farm land with a house or two scattered about as they drove. In a couple of miles, Ginger spotted a trailer park and patted Larry's arm to get his attention. "I can't wait," he said, smiling at her.

Jesse looked over at Ava, and she was gazing out at the scenery as they passed by. He looked at Kat, and she was fiddling with a cassette player someone had given her for the road. She pushed play and the spindles turned, but it was silent. She shook it but still no sound. She turned it around and found that the volume was down.

As the cassette turned and the sound went up Kat began to sing along to Journey's *Don't Stop Believing* and looked up at Jesse. He smiled and began to sing with her, causing Ava to lean forward and stare at them as they swayed their heads and sang a verse to one another.

The moment was quickly over; Jesse had to slow down for stalled cars blocking the road. He weaved in and out of them and noticed it was like that as far as the eye could see. "It could take us a while to get home at this pace."

"Do you think we'll make it by Christmas?" Ava asked.

"At this speed over about five hundred miles, that's probably about two days. But we still have to find some gas somewhere in about a hundred and fifty miles," Jesse explained. "We can siphon some from the stalled cars once we make room in our tank. So by Christmas, Ava, it's certainly doable."

"That's good, because I want Santa to be able to come, and I want to hang up a stocking. It's not that I still believe in Santa anymore, it's just…My parents always hung one up for me. When I got up on Christmas morning that was the very first thing I did, check my stocking. I want that to remember them by," she declared.

Kat patted her on the knee and said, "We'll hang a stocking."

They rolled passed a group of teenagers busting windows out of cars in a store parking lot. Jesse tapped on the rear window and pointed. Ginger reached for her shotgun and held it in her lap. They began to see more and more people meandering around as they passed through some small towns. Some were in their yards, some were on their porch, and some were bent over under a car hood. They would generally just stop and watch as they drove by, probably wondering how their truck was running. But when they passed by a Walmart Super Center, there were several armed men out front and a huge line of people that weaved all around the parking lot. "What do you think is happening over there?" Kat asked.

"Looks like they may be rationing the merchandise or selling it to the highest bidder," Jesse guessed. He kept his pace as he continued to drive around the still automobiles that blocked the road, preventing them from traveling at any sort of speed over twenty miles per hour.

They passed by a small gas station that had all the windows busted out. Two men were fighting in front over what looked like a twelve pack of beer. They tugged back and forth on the box until it finally burst open and cans spilled out, rupturing several and spraying them with the foamy liquid. Another business had been burned to the ground. A fire truck and two police cars sat in the parking lot abandoned and also partially burned. Jesse pointed them out and said, "That fire might have happened at the same time the storm hit. The fire truck and police cars must have died."

The cars began to get thinner as they drove farther out into more farming country, and they were able to pick up the pace to about thirty-five miles an hour. Most of the cars had pulled over to the side of the road when they stalled but there were several that just sat in the way. Jesse said, "Alright, it's getting better." As soon as he said that, he slammed on the brakes as two off-road go-carts tore across in front of the truck and disappeared into the woods. He looked back at Ginger and Larry, and they seemed to be fine, so he proceeded slowly down the highway only to discover just around the next curve that it was blocked. He stopped the truck about a hundred yards away, and they all gawked at a Boeing 777 that had crash landed and ended up across the lanes, blocking the road. The plane stretched across the four lanes lying on its belly and the one wing in their view was partially torn off. The asphalt was crumpled up around the nose where it had dug in, leaving a trench behind the fuselage.

"Would you look at that?" Kat panted

"Wow! Is that your plane?" Ava asked, astonished by the sight.

"No, that's not our plane," Jesse answered, stunned at what he was looking at.

Ginger and Larry's mouths hung open as they stared through the open back glass of the truck and beheld the mammoth of a plane that blocked their way. Out from around the jumbo jet came the two go-carts and about ten heavily armed men. Jesse looked at Kat, and Kat looked at Jesse. "Ava, we might not make it by Christmas," Kat gulped.

"Fee-fi-fo-fum, what will be this outcome," Larry groaned.

# Afterword

Into another predicament, the characters find themselves as chaos begins to unfold in their unknown world. Isn't that how life is, chaotic and unknown? I know that there were some deep subjects dealt with in this story, but it was to provoke thought and reflection of our own lives as we lived through theirs. I know that I felt for each one as I became them. I cried as their struggles became real to me. Their loss brought pain and I wept over each death. I became angry at the evil that took place and was enraged at the heinous crimes committed. I laughed at their wit, and felt their confidence, and their insecurities. And in the midst of it all, we find love.

My intention was to be as real as I could without succumbing to the filth that already engulfs our world. My goal was that you related to at least one character and you became their cheerleader as their story unfolded. Maybe you can look past some of my indiscretions with forgiveness, which may have come to light while you read this book. Find out what happens to Jesse, Kat, Larry, Ginger and Ava in the winter of 2018, as their story continues. Thank you, for giving me your attention for a while, and I hope you were entertained.

Vince Byrd

August 30, 2017

# About the Author

Vince Byrd always put pen to paper to express himself, from loves letters to his wife, songs he would write and plunk out on his guitar, to even some poetry. Vince is also published in *Love is a Verb, Upper Room,* and has published a children's book called *Donnie Doo-Doos.* He enjoys collecting toys from his childhood and makes his living by selling all kinds of things online, including toys. Vince resides in Acworth, Georgia with his wife Angie.

Follow me on facebook.com

www.ingramcontent.com/pod-product-compliance
Lightning Source LLC
Chambersburg PA
CBHW060054150626
46556CB00017BA/677